Praise for
Madame Dorion:
Her Journey to the Oregon Country

"This journal of Marie Dorion (1786 – 1850) by Lenora Rain-Lee Good is an account of a largely unknown Indian woman whose fortitude and perseverance is unsurpassed in early American History. Written from Marie's perspective, the author does an excellent job of weaving Marie's thoughts into the storyline and still maintains a high level of historical accuracy."

–Ned Eddins, historian and author
www.TheFurTrapper.com

"As the author notes, Sacagawea had a better public relations firm working on her behalf than did the subject of this fine historical novel. But Marie Dorion, a remarkable Indian woman who traveled across the continent with the first big expedition after Lewis and Clark returned, has a strong supporter in her corner through the lyrical words of Lenora Good. It pleases me that more people will discover the amazing life of Marie who unlike Sacagawea remained in the Northwest leaving a legacy of generosity and care for family and community. May this book reach the hands of many – especially the young – to experience a true heroine's journey."

–Jane Kirkpatrick, Bestselling author of *A Name of her Own*

Madame Dorion

Her Journey
to the Oregon Country

MADAME DORION

HER JOURNEY
TO THE OREGON COUNTRY

A HISTORICAL NOVEL BY

LENORA RAIN-LEE GOOD

S & H Publishing, Inc.
Purcellville, VA USA

Published by S & H Publishing, Inc.

P O Box 456, Purcellville, VA 20134

ISBN-10: 1633200051

ISBN-13: 978-1-63320-005-0

Ebook ISBN: 978-1-63320-006-7

For my sister Marjorie,
and my friend Ned,
who gave unstintingly
of their time, their knowledge,
and their encouragement.

"**...and thus we starved in view of plenty.**"
—Warren Angus Ferris, *Life in the Rocky Mountains*

Contents

THE JOURNEY

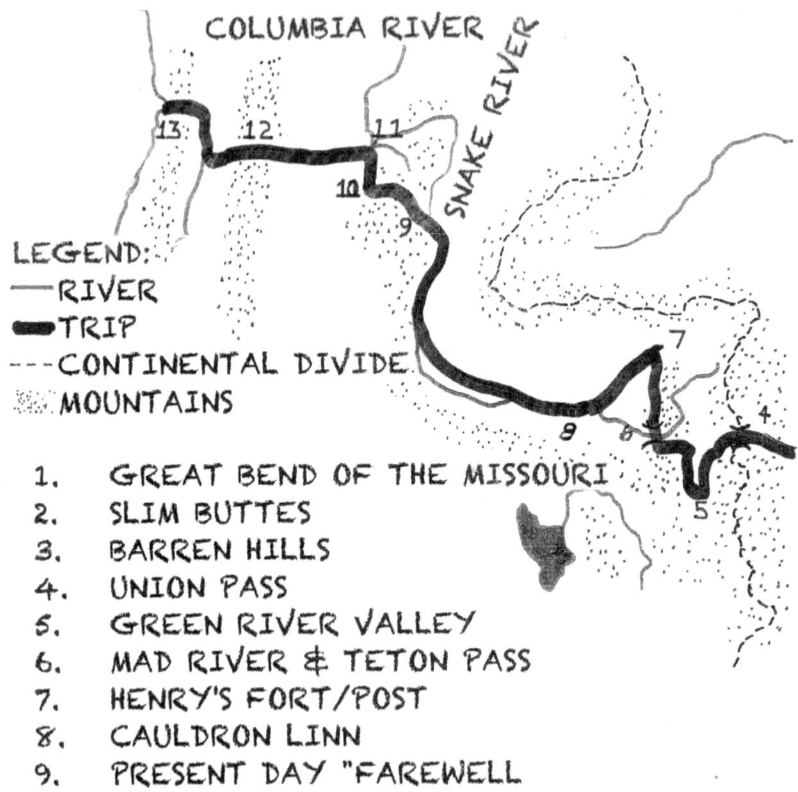

1. GREAT BEND OF THE MISSOURI
2. SLIM BUTTES
3. BARREN HILLS
4. UNION PASS
5. GREEN RIVER VALLEY
6. MAD RIVER & TETON PASS
7. HENRY'S FORT/POST
8. CAULDRON LINN
9. PRESENT DAY "FAREWELL BEND" START OF "HELL'S CANYON"
10. VILLAGE OF SCIATOGAS & TUSHEPAKS
11. WALLULA & WALLA WALLA RIVER
12. GREAT FALLS OF THE COLUMBIA
13. FORT ASTORIA

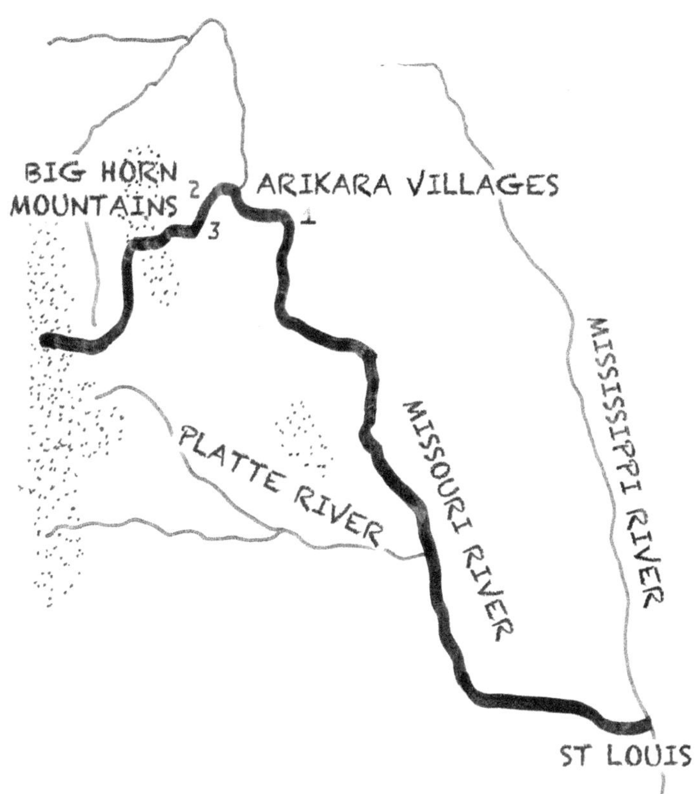

BASED ON MAP, AND USED WITH
PERMISSION, BY O. NED EDDINS
WWW.THEFURTRAPPER.COM

Preface

Madame Marie Dorion was an Indian woman, born around 1786, who made the extraordinarily difficult journey from St. Louis to present-day Astoria, Oregon, five years after the famous Lewis and Clark expedition. However, because Marie did not have the same degree of public relations that her counterpart, Sacajawea, had while traveling with Lewis and Clark, very little is actually known about her life. As history provided so little factual information to work with, I have used fictive techniques to frame my interpretation of Marie's experiences. One thing we can be pretty sure of: as an Indian woman, she would have been quiet and stoic and relatively accepting of whatever life handed her, though she did have her moments.

We know Marie could neither read nor write, and to that end, this journal of her travels to the Oregon Country is purely fiction; however, we do know she made the journey with her husband, two boys, and the Wilson Price Hunt party, also known as the Astorians. John Jacob Astor, a real estate investor, fur trader, and leading businessman of the day, became the founder of the American Fur Company in 1808. He hired Hunt to lead an expedition of trappers to Fort Astor in present-day Astoria, Oregon.

With the exception of Hunt and the two Dorion boys, all the men were mountain men—they were trappers and hunters familiar with the woods and survival therein. (Marie was also well-educated in that field.) Beaver furs were highly prized for men's hats; however the hides of other animals—bear, buffalo, deer, elk, wolf, any fur that could be taken and properly dressed for shipment back east, either by ship or overland, were welcome and brought money.

A number of men on that expedition kept journals, including Hunt, who kept several. Only one of them, the one that dealt with our portion of the journey, remains extant; it has been translated from French to English and is available online. (French was almost a second language in the America of that day; the "intelligentsia" who wrote for and desired publication almost exclusively wrote in French. The other journals, written by the mountain men, were in English or have also been translated.) Marie's journal entries are based on those journals I could find and read.

I have woven several other fictions into Marie's writings. Four of these are described below.

Fiction Number One

Becoming literate. Marie's Indian name, if not entirely lost to history, is pretty well hidden. Today, we know her as Madame Marie Dorion. She was a member of the Ioway tribe, and though she was undoubtedly very intelligent, there is no record of her ever learning to read or write. How could she keep a journal if she could neither write nor even read? I made it up.

And how did she become literate, living with Indians, whose culture was entirely oral, and semi-literate mountain men? Enter Father Lark (I made him up, too). Jesuits were all over the Missouri River country at that time; missionary priests brought their religion and particular brand of European civilization, along with the French language. It seems reasonable to me that Marie's village would have had at least one resident priest.

The Jesuits were not only missionaries, but as today, they were also rebels of a sort. The Jesuits were, and still are, the best educated and most liberal of any priests in the Roman Catholic Church. I can easily visualize a priest like Father Lark, who would enjoy teaching an inquisitive, intelligent Indian girl to read and write, especially if he thought she might enter the convent, which Marie did not, or there would be no story to tell—or a very different story.

Fiction Number Two

The Prodigy Son. Marie had two sons at the time of this story, Jean Baptiste and Paul, both born before her trip began. We know little about either, but we do know Paul was sickly. As I began imagining Marie's journal (remember, she never actually wrote one), Paul took on a life of his own, becoming a child prodigy in the spiritual clothing of a shaman or medicine man. In fact, he nearly took over my imagination *and* the story of his mother.

Fiction Number Three

The Journal itself. Marie was very intelligent. She learned, spoke, and translated just about every language she heard and, in acting as translator, became a valued member of the group later called the Astorians (so named because their goal was Fort Astoria, on the Pacific coast of Oregon).

But she left us not one word of what she thought, what

she experienced, what she hoped, what she feared, what her joys or sorrows were. She left us nothing of her life. Therefore, just about everything in her journal is how *I think* she might have reacted to any given situation, how *I think* she might have acted or behaved.

A note on the dates. Where I use the Moon Dates, it's fiction about things I'm pretty sure happened but don't know when, or even where. Where I use actual calendar dates, those dates, as well as the kernel of her entry, came from actual journals written by some of the men on the journey, including Wilson Price Hunt.

Fiction Number Four

My Efforts. I wish I could claim it was terribly hard work gathering the few facts I could glean, and trying to knit them together into an interesting story, but it was really fun. I loved reading the various spare accounts and fleeting mentions of Marie I was able to find and trying to figure out which were accurate and which were not.

Thanks to the scarcity of factual information, I gave up trying to keep the journal strictly factual and decided to take what little I do know of Marie's history — the parts that made sense to me — and have fun writing a story I hope you will enjoy.

Marie Dorion was a woman I would like to have known. Marie became, in a sense, my alter ego. And Paul? I hope that, in whatever heaven he resides, he finds and reads a copy of this story and that he enjoys it as much as I do. I admit it: I am in love with Paul.

PART I

MARRIAGE

1804–1811

No. 1 - *Corn Festival Moon, 1804*

Write your life.

That is what Father Lark said, but I do not know what to write. Father Lark gave me this little empty book when I told him I would marry the younger Pierre Dorion. He was saddened I chose to marry Pierre rather than to go into the convent and marry God, but I had not yet been baptized in his church, and the idea of marrying a god who would not hold me in his arms or put babies in my belly did not sound like much fun.

Father Lark first came to our village when I was a child living in the tipi of my mother. He was not the first priest to come to our village, but he was the most fun. The others were old, and serious, and interested in saving our souls, but not in laughing or winning friends.

I was with a group of children as we played by the river, enjoying the warmth of the sun and all the ripe berries we could stuff in our mouths, when down the river came three canoes. Two of the canoes held men from our village. The third carried a Black Robe who not only paddled his own canoe but, in a most beautiful and happy voice, sang *Alouette, gentille alouette, Alouette, je te plumerai.* The song was not new to us; all the Frenchmen who visited sang it, but the sight of a Black Robe paddling his own canoe? *That* was different!

Coming close to shore, when the Black Robe saw us, he

waved and smiled, and when he landed at our village we ran to see him. He unfolded from the canoe into a tall man. Never had I seen such a tall man! His skin seemed stretched and barely able to cover his bones, and his robe was too short in length and in the sleeves.

His hair was blacker than his robes, his eyes bluer than any sky. He laughed, and called us to him, and asked us our names. He spoke each name as many times as it took for him to say it correctly, and after that, he matched the right face to our names and called us by the names our parents gave us. As people became baptized, he gave them a new name, a French or Christian name.

This priest loved to sing and to whistle. He could mimic bird calls as well as any of our men, so we called him Father Lark. He liked the name so much he introduced himself to any who came to visit as Father Lark. Whatever his real name was, once he settled in our village, he never used it, in favor of Father Lark.

My mother often told me I was too much like a boy, curious about everything. Watching Father Lark write in the book he called his journal, I asked if he would teach me to write. He thought it was a good idea and said he would teach any child who wanted to learn to read and write as long as their parents did not mind.

We gathered near his lodging, excited and eager to learn, at least in the beginning. But learning was hard, and most of the children stopped coming because of that, or because their parents needed them to help. My father said he had enough boys to help him and, as long as my mother did not mind, I could attend the school.

The old priest wanted me to be baptized if I was going

to attend the school, but Father Lark said one should not be bribed into being baptized. I said I would probably be baptized someday, but not now. Father Lark said it would be necessary before I could continue my education at the convent. But that would be many moons in the future.

No. 2 - *Corn Festival Moon, 1804*

Every year during the Heat Moon the Dorion men came down the Missouri River, or Muddy as we call it, on their barges and rafts which carried hides and bear grease the men had collected through the winter. They always stopped for a day or two at our village on the way to Saint Louis. If any of our men had hides to sell, the Dorion men would take them and bring the money or trade goods with them when they returned home.

The Dorion boy, Pierre, would always come find me. If I had a bit of beadwork ready, he would take it to trade, and bring me back more beads, or perhaps a ribbon for my hair. Pierre is older than I, and I must have appeared very silly and childish, but he never lost patience with me. He allowed me to accompany him when he visited our village, and he often requested me as a guide. He knew our village very well, but I was happy to spend time with him. He made me feel necessary and important. He wanted to be with *me*.

This year, when the Dorions came, Pierre's papa was not with them. My father feared he had died, but Pierre said he had gone a ways upriver with the white men who came through earlier, Messrs. Lewis and Clark.

I had finished a vest with fancy beadwork, and Pierre

thought it would bring much money in Saint Louis. In return, I asked for red cloth, if there was enough money. Pierre thought there would be. He smiled and told me he was sure there would be enough for me to make a skirt and a blouse, that I should not worry.

He called me his Little Marie and asked to speak to my parents in private. Never before had he asked me to leave. Never before had he called me his. Did it mean what I hoped and dreamed it might mean?

It did! When the men returned to the village yesterday, Pierre asked me to marry him, and my parents gave their permission. Father Lark said he would come to the feast, but he could not marry us, as I was not yet baptized and the banns had not been read.

No. 3 - *Corn Festival Moon, 1804*

All day, on the day of our wedding feast, Pierre seemed to ignore me, but whenever I looked at him, a huge grin covered his face. More than once I thought his face would split in half like an over-ripe melon.

Everyone brought food to share, and the whole village came to the feast, even Father Lark, who joined in the singing and dancing. Earlier, Pierre had given me enough red cloth for both a blouse and a skirt. At the feast, he gave me a ribbon to wear with the new outfit I would make. But the biggest surprise was his gift to me: for my Pierre had bought, and now wore, the vest I gave him to sell in Saint Louis. This made me know he valued my work, and me.

Though Father Lark could not marry us, he blessed us and wished us many children and many years of happiness. I thought he might be sorry that I had not chosen to marry his God and go to live in the convent, but Father Lark said marriage was a calling and he was happy for Pierre and me.

The nights began to turn chilly as my husband and I traveled north to the home of his mother. The bucks began to grow their new antlers. Grandfather Sky roared his approval as he pushed the clouds across the plains.

As often as possible, my Pierre and I slept out under the stars. When rain threatened, I set up the tipi for his brothers, with whom we journeyed, and us. Our supplies were packed on the horses the men bought in Saint Louis so we had little to carry. Pierre and I walked at the end of the group, just the two of us, slow enough we could be alone with each other.

I decided I liked to sleep in the arms of my husband—how I like to say that, to call my Pierre my husband!—more than I would like to sleep alone with an unseen god.

No. 4 - Corn Festival Moon, 1804

We walked and rode several days from my village on the Platte River to the home of my new mother, Holy Rainbow, who lives where the James River empties into the Muddy. It was a good time for my Pierre and me to get to know each other—and for me to learn a little about avoiding his temper.

Pierre's parents live in a wood house and do not travel with the seasons. His brothers sleep outside in good weather or in front of the fire in bad. I do not like the cabin, as it is dark and smoky, and when the men drink and fight, it is loud. My Pierre and I sleep in our own tipi near his parents' home.

There is cold in the air, and tonight under the full moon, Holy Rainbow and I will harvest the last of the Three Sisters—the corn, beans, and squash—that she planted last spring and will store them so the squirrels and mice will not get into them.

Old Dorion, or Papa Pierre, as he wishes me to call him, has returned from his sojourn with the Lewis and Clark people. He told many stories, but mostly, he wanted to be alone with Holy Rainbow. When he first returned, he made the boys leave the cabin and sleep outside. They tried to move into the tipi with Pierre and me, but Pierre said they could not. Now, however they are back inside. How do they breathe the smoke-filled air? How does Holy Rainbow put up with the loudness, the constant bickering and fighting? I do not much like it!

Papa Pierre thinks it is silly that I learned to read and write, but Holy Rainbow thinks it is smart. She has told my Pierre that I am intelligent, that he should pay attention to what I say, and to let me read any contracts he makes before he writes his name. My Pierre can read and write a little, but he would rather study trail sign than books—or contracts for work.

More than two moons have passed since Papa Pierre returned, and today Holy Rainbow and I spent time getting the cabin ready to leave and the packs ready for the horses. Tomorrow, we start out on a hunting trip to kill enough animals so we will have meat for the winter and to help the men start with their trapping. Once we have enough meat, she and I will return to the cabin to smoke it, make jerky and pemmican, and work on the hides we will bring back with us. The men will continue to hunt and then return for the provisions we make before setting out on their winter trapping expedition.

This trip will be the first time I have been away from my Pierre. I will treat him with his favorite foods to take on this trip, so he will not forget me while he is gone all winter. Or return home with another woman.

No. 5 - *Cold Moon, 1805*

The men have been gone since before the long night, and most of the people of the tribe of Holy Rainbow were gone before that. She and I are alone in the cabin, our only company the wolves that prowl about at night. Sometimes they come up to the cabin; we see the prints they make in the snow when we go out for water and wood in the morning.

Yesterday, as we approached the river to check our traps and get water, we heard a wolf snarl and growl. My new mother ordered me to stay back as she held her spear ready to use. I drew my knife from the scabbard and walked by her side. I would not allow her to walk into danger alone. She smiled when she realized I, too, carried a weapon.

A big he-wolf was caught in one of our traps! He was the largest wolf I had ever seen. His mouth was bloody where he had tried to chew his leg through so he could escape the trap. He stood, growled, and lunged at us as we approached. The chain on the trap stopped him mid-lunge, and he fell onto his side, howling in pain and rage. Holy Rainbow walked close enough to spear him through his heart.

He was a brave wolf and gave us a thick pelt. I got the water while she skinned him. We used the meat to bait the other traps and took the hide back to the cabin. Holy Rainbow will tan it and should get a good price for it this summer in Saint Louis, as the fur is thick, a beautiful dark gray with silver tips.

Earlier in the fall, we had killed two porcupines and dyed the quills. I have been using them to sew fancy work on a shirt for my Pierre, a design similar to the one on his vest. Holy Rainbow and I share the work, but I enjoy sewing and bead work more than she, so she works on the hides and I do the fancy work.

Although the cabin is warm and comfortable, it is dark and sometimes smoky. I miss the lightness of our tipi, and I miss my husband. Holy Rainbow and I talk often of our men and wonder how they are doing. We lament how far away is spring, and how long the days before our men return. The days are shorter, the nights are longer, and Holy Rainbow and I are alone with only each other and our thoughts for company.

Holy Rainbow has shown me some of the traditional designs from her tribe, and I am working them, mixed with my own designs, into moccasins for Pierre. Holy Rainbow likes what I have done and is using some of my tribal designs in her beadwork. When she does beadwork. She has been making the moccasins and giving them to me to add the beads. It is good we like each other and get along well.

When my Pierre returns, I will ask him to build us a cabin close to the cabin of his mother.

No. 6 - *Warm Moon, 1805*

The ground is no longer frozen, and when the men return with their hides and grease, Holy Rainbow and I will be busy getting ready to leave with them on the trip to Saint Louis to sell the hides we have gathered and whatever the men bring home.

Yesterday, we watched the birds fly from the south to the north to feed on the worms of the fields, a sure sign Grandmother Earth wakes, and warm weather comes. Their songs are welcome. Surely, they will call our men home.

During the day, we leave the cabin door open to let in the sunshine and fresh air. Our hides are packed and ready to load onto the barges. All we need now are our men, and the hides and grease they will bring to sell.

The big question we ask ourselves now is, will the brothers bring wives back with them? Did they winter with a village, or on their own in the deep woods? Will my Pierre bring another woman?

I can hardly wait for my Pierre to come home. When he does, I will set up our tipi so we may be alone and get to know each other again. It is hard, when night comes, to sleep in the cabin. I so want my Pierre here, in my arms.

Holy Rainbow's people have returned to make camp by the river. It is good to have friends around, and children running and playing. It is good to hear stories and laughter. Yesterday, the children played a game of tag, and one of the boys chased a girl who fell into the river when the bank gave way. By happy chance, some men fished nearby and were able to save her from the fast waters. We are all very grateful she was pulled back onto the shore and only scared, wet, and cold. Children are too valuable to lose.

Both Holy Rainbow and I agree that it is good to eat the cooking of someone else. We take some of our food and give to a neighbor and, in return, are given bowls of stew and bread that we did not have to make.

Now, if only Papa and my Pierre and the boys would hurry and come home.

No. 7 - *Flower Moon, 1805*

I have been a bride for almost a year, and my husband has been gone during the cold months, when I most needed his warmth.

Holy Rainbow thinks the men will be home soon. Everything we can do has been done. We have tanned our hides, planted the Three Sisters, and only use the wood to cook with. Holy Rainbow smiles as I walk to the door and look out, again and again, searching for our men.

I thought Father Lark had come to visit. I heard someone singing his song, *Alouette*, yesterday and ran outside, dumping quills and a shirt on the floor. It was two Métis in a canoe coming down the James. I asked if they had seen my Pierre; they shook their heads and kept going.

It was too much sadness. I returned to the cabin, and while I bent over to pick up my scattered mess, tears began to drop from my eyes. Holy Rainbow said nothing but knelt next to me and put her arms around me until the tears stopped. She complimented me that while my tears fell, she heard not a sob. I smiled at that, for I do not know of a single tribe in which crying is allowed, except for mourning. And that should be done in private.

I vowed to myself to not cry again. Ever. It is not fitting for the wife of Pierre Dorion the Younger to cry except at his death. And he will not die for many, many years. We will be old and gray when we die. It is not fitting for a person of my tribe to cry. I am, truly, shamed.

No. 8 - *Flower Moon, 1805*

The strawberries are nearly ripe. As always, I wonder if there will be enough for us, the deer, and the birds. The bright-colored and chattering queets are here, and they love the berries as much as we do. I am mostly worried that Papa and my Pierre will not make it home in time to eat any, as Holy Rainbow and I eat them as fast as we find them.

Before Holy Rainbow left to visit in the village, she helped me set up our tipi, which has been packed away in the rafters of the cabin. It is good to sit in my own home again.

The cabin is nice, but it is not mine. Perhaps, someday, my Pierre will make me my own cabin. I would like that, especially if it is near the home of his mother.

The sleeping hides and blankets were in the sun all day yesterday, and they smell fresh and ready for my husband's return. Holy Rainbow is busy preparing the cabin for Papa Pierre's homecoming. While it is quiet, and no one is yet here, I will write in my journal.

O! I hear shrieking! Holy Rainbow yells and calls out to her husband. Our men are home!

No. 9 - *Rose Moon, 1805*

They brought several hides, and many pounds of buffalo and bear grease and tallow, but no women. Now they make barges to carry all the hides and grease and tallow down the river while Holy Rainbow and I work on the hides to get them ready for market.

My husband says I have too much to do to spend time writing in my journal. Perhaps he is right. He tells me I will get to go with them and visit my parents if I would like, while he and the men go to Saint Louis. Oh, to see my mother again! He says I can write then, if I want.

No. 10 - *Strawberry Moon, 1805*

We arrived at the home of my mother to discover great sadness. Father died of a bad cough during the Cold Moon. I miss his laugh and his love.

When I asked Mother if Father Lark had come, she said Father had not wanted a Black Robe to see him. But, she hastened to add, Father Lark *did* come for her and gave her a great deal of comfort, even if it was outside the tipi, where Father would not see.

Mother led Pierre and me to where Father is buried.

We laid down tobacco for his spirit and ribbons for his hair. I tied a piece of the red cloth that he and I both loved to the tree branch that shaded him.

That night, Mother pointed to my flat belly and asked if I was happy. Both my Pierre and I laughed, and he told her he did his best. Mother used her pretend-stern voice to tell him that, since I was not yet with child, his best was, obviously, not very good and that she would not change her mind until she could hold a grandchild in her arms. My Pierre tried to convince her he did his very best, but she only grunted. Then she smiled and served us food.

The tribe held a feast for us that night, and several of the tribe brought Papa Pierre or his sons various pelts to take to Saint Louis to sell. Some of the younger men asked to come with us to see the city and do their own trading.

Two days later, when our barge swept out into the river, I traveled with my husband. It was hard to leave my mother, but I, too, wanted to see the city of the white men. I had heard it described so often, that there were many buildings with glass windows and stores filled with wonders.

And, I admit, I wanted to do my best to keep my Pierre away from the firewater. When he and his brothers drank it, they became loud and fought with each other and with anyone else who was near.

No. 11 - Thunder Moon, 1805

I did not care for Saint Louis. The streets were dirty, there were too many people, and they were loud. They yelled all the time! No one, except those of the Tribes that I saw, and a few trappers, spoke in a normal voices. Compared to Saint Louis, the home of Holy Rainbow, even filled with our lively men, is quiet.

We lived, for the time we were in Saint Louis, in the cabin of Papa Dorion's friend. The wife of his friend was American—and loud. She and her husband drank firewater and continually offered it to my Pierre and to me. When he drank it, Pierre became mean and angry. I did not drink any and tried to tell her not to offer it, but she did not speak French. And in trying to talk to me, she yelled even more, as if that would help me understand what she said. She laughed often and slapped her thigh when she laughed the loudest, but I do not know what was funny. I wondered if her thigh was bruised from all the slapping. I was very glad to leave her loud laughter behind us.

We sold everything, even the barges, and Pierre bought me beads and blue cloth. Papa Pierre bought yellow cloth for Holy Rainbow. There was enough of each for us to share. Again, my Pierre and I walked to the home of his mother. This time, he spent more time with the men, and Holy Rainbow and I walked together. The men would not let us walk at the end, unprotected, so we walked close to the front and gathered whatever berries and greens we came upon. There was much laughter on this walk as we told our stories of Saint Louis to each other. And then we reached the James River.

It is good to be home. The summer storms seemed louder than usual, and the thunder boomed right over our heads. I think I like being in the cabin now, especially when the rains come down so hard, like the love of my good husband when he is with me.

The corn is up and will be ready for harvesting soon. The berries are ripe, and Holy Rainbow and I are busy picking berries, cooking some, eating some, and drying some. We also fish and smoke whatever fish we do not eat that day to take with us.

Pierre tells me he wants me to come with him for the winter trapping. He values my knowledge of the woods, he says. He also says he is tired of sleeping cold and alone in the snow. He says I can bring my journal, if I want, though I may not have time to write in it.

When I asked Holy Rainbow if she was coming too, she smiled and told me she would come only if her man asked. She does not like the cold that much. She admitted she actually likes her time alone in the cabin.

No. 12 - *Beaver Moon, 1805*

We have traveled many days to the north and east. It is very cold, and the men are happy to have one more person along to help with cooking and setting up the camp. While they hunt, I make the shelter out of branches, overlay it with hides brought for this purpose, and get the fire going. We all sleep inside. The hides help keep the heat in, especially when snow falls and covers them. My Pierre and I share our blankets and sleep warm in each other's arms.

We had been encamped for almost two moons when I told my husband that it seems his best is very good, after all. He looked at me as if I spoke a different language. When I smiled and told him that our mothers would be grandmothers next summer, probably during the Moon of the Strawberry, maybe sooner, he let out a loud whoop, picked me up, and twirled me around, laughing and yelling and spinning until we were both dizzy and fell in the snow. He was careful to fall so I was on top of him and not injured.

Then when he sobered, he said he should not have brought me after all. It was my turn to laugh. I told him that if I had not come, I would not be with child. Besides, Ioway women are used to having children and working hard, and I am, after all, an Ioway woman.

He again started yelling with joy and saying that I was the woman of Pierre Dorion, about to become a Papa! He picked me up and swung me around again and again, all the time yelling that his best was good enough. He has already decided I will give him a son, and we shall call him Jean Baptiste after two of his brothers.

Being with child in the winter is good. The extra body inside means extra warmth for the mother. I did not suffer from the cold and ice as the men did. And they made sure I had the choice piece of meat on my plate. One with a little fat to keep me healthy.

No. 13 - *Cold Moon, 1806*

Several wolves with thick pelts and deep voices came too close to our camp and have been killed by the men. Some were shot, others trapped. Not one is as large as the one Holy Rainbow killed last winter, though all have thick pelts and will bring high prices.

The Long Night has passed, and it is a new year. I cooked

a special stew for the men in celebration. Papa Pierre gave me a hat he made from the head of one of the wolves. The ears are still on it, so when I wear it, I look like a she-wolf. My husband tells everyone that I am as ferocious as a she-wolf with cubs, so they must be wary of me.

It is too cold to hold my quill and write anything but short entries. I write while the men are out, so my Pierre does not see me do it. I am also busy with the hides and cooking.

No. 14 - Warm Moon, 1806

The earth is warmer in my hands. The trees feel warmer when I touch them, and green replaces the white of snow and the brown of mud. Or at least covers the mud with new growth. We are going home.

My belly is bulging, though not yet big. I can feel little Jean Baptiste moving. My Pierre is not sure if he has felt his son move yet.

The horses are taking their time, eating the new growth as it comes up. All but one of them made it through the winter. The one that died, we ate. And took his hide.

We have a record number of pelts, and Papa Pierre says never has he had so much grease and tallow. All the horses are heavily loaded, so we will walk.

All the men have new moccasins, each with a little beadwork on them. Papa Pierre says we will be home in another moon or so. Our last stop will be to check and collect the beaver traps as we make our way home. We will eat beaver tail for dinner. The only thing better than beaver tail is buffalo hump, which we will hunt as we walk back to our home.

My fingers are warm enough to hold the quill but too swollen with Jean Baptiste, or Jean-Jean as I already call him, that I think I will not write much until he is in my arms. That will make my Pierre happy.

No. 15 - Rose Moon, 1806

My Pierre wanted me to come down on the barge to see my mother, to show her how good a man he was. She was very happy and even came with us to Saint Louis. I am glad she did, because her help is needed. In the village, everyone helps to raise a child, but in Saint Louis, it is different.

We again stayed with the American friends. This time Anna, as I hear her name, is not so loud. I think because she yelled at my mother, and my mother yelled back. Or, maybe, it is little Jean-Jean. When anyone yells, he jumps. Anna loves to hold him and sing to him, and is teaching me some words in English. It is funny to watch my mother and Anna squabble, quietly, over who will hold the baby. I am totally forgotten and ignored, except when he is hungry. Only then do they allow me to hold my child.

My Pierre rushed into the cabin, more excited than I have seen him since I told him I was with child. He grabbed my hand and pulled me, "Come. Come see. It is a present from Papa and me. Come. Look."

He practically dragged me down the street, he was in such a hurry. Then he stopped in front of a small house. His face beamed. "It is ours," he said. "Papa thought we should have our own place, and he bought it for us. Well, for us and the family."

He opened the door, and inside were two beds, a table, three chairs, a stove, and a shelf for dishes. "Do you not think this grand?" He was so excited, he could barely contain himself, "Look! It has windows, unlike Mother's. And a proper stove for you to cook on. Do you not love it, my Marie? Is it not grand?"

My heart fell. I knew if I moved I would step on it.

My Pierre must have seen the change in my face because he quickly asked me, his voice filled with concern, "Marie? My Marie, what is it? What is wrong?"

I looked at him, the tears I vowed never to shed again pooling close to the surface, and asked him if this meant he did not want me to come along on the hunting trips any more. Did it mean I would never get to see Holy Rainbow again?

He exploded in laughter. When he calmed down, he told me that of course I would go hunting with him. And with his brothers. That, after all, I am a part of the Trappers Dorion, and he had no intention of ever leaving me home again for any reason.

Then he took me in his arms and said he did not like sleeping alone, especially in the cold.

Why, I asked him, are there two beds?

He smiled, and said one was for my mother when she came to visit, and for Jean-Jean when he was older, or for the brothers, when they were in town.

I am not happy about this. There is too much firewater here in Saint Louis. But I am only a wife; what can I do? I would rather be with my man than back in the tipi of my mother.

No. 16 - Corn Moon, 1807

Jean-Jean continues to grow and is healthy. He was a good boy on the hunting trip, and my Pierre says he brought us much luck, as we brought back more hides than ever before. Papa and the brothers agreed.

We have been home since the Rose Moon. Papa returned to his home and Holy Rainbow. We stayed in our cabin. The Expedition headed by the Americans Lewis and Clark came through town to much celebration. They traveled across the Big Mountains and down the Columbia River to the Pacific Ocean.

These were the men Papa Pierre went with, for a while. When they came to town on their way back, my Pierre talked many hours with the men, getting directions and trail markings. Does he plan on such a trip? Or, like many trappers, is this just his way of building knowledge in case he ever needs it?

They had a French Canadian guide, Toussaint Charbonneau, who brought along his wife, Sacajawea, and their young son. I did not meet her. Their son is named Jean Baptiste, but they call him Pomp. These Frenchmen have no imagination when it comes to naming their children or their wives.

My little Jean-Jean now walks and says words. He was very good on the hunting trip, pointing at things and looking at his father or me for the word. He is quiet and does not scream like the American children. How can American mothers not train their children to be quiet? Do they not fear their enemies?

He is refusing the breast more and more, and wants to

eat from his father's plate. My Pierre is very patient and cuts the pieces very small. He is not always as patient with me, but as long as he is patient with his children, I will be happy.

The little one is waking from his nap, so I must close for now. I hope not to be so long in writing again. I see and hear many things I tell myself to remember, then when I sit to write, they are forgotten, like the chatter of the bright and flitting queets that fill our summer days with sound and color.

No. 17 - Thunder Moon, 1808

The baby is not due for a long time, but I am sicker than I was with little Jean-Jean. I hope it is not a sign the baby is going to be sick. My Pierre is delighted and hopes this time I will have a girl. I am too sick to care.

We had another good year and brought home more hides and grease than ever before. Papa and the brothers are sure it is my Jean-Jean and me who call the animals to the traps. At least that is what they say. They call Jean-Jean the One Who Calls Animals to the Traps of the Dorions. It is a very long name for such a small boy. He will have much growing to do before he can wear that name and not have to drag it in the dust like a toy.

The air is hot and filled with moisture. Clouds are on the horizon, and at night we can see the lightning. Sometimes the clouds are overhead and the heat becomes oppressive, and the Thunder God rolls and rumbles above us and throws his spears of lightning to flash and crack. It is always a time of fear out in the grass, for fires can burn hot and fast.

Little Jean-Jean helps as much as he can, especially when his papa works as a guide or interpreter. I would like to go back to Holy Rainbow to live, but Pierre wants to live in Saint Louis where there is work to be had.

No. 18 - *Hunter's Moon, 1808*

Jean-Jean is very excited to be going. As soon as my Pierre comes home from his guide job, we will leave.

My Pierre still wants me to come hunting with him, and I pack what we will need for us. We should leave in three days, if my Pierre is home. I fear it will be a long time before I write again. I hope I do not forget how.

I think Father Lark was wrong when he said I would go places and meet people and have adventures; I lead a very normal and rather dull life. Perhaps he thought the life of an Ioway woman was exciting. He should get married, and then he would learn.

I am very tired. This baby drains me of energy. It will be born while we hunt. I hope my Pierre will be there, and I will not be in the camp alone.

No. 19 - *Rose Moon, 1809*

Paul came during the Hunger Moon. As sick as I had been, I expected a hard birth, but he slipped into this world easily and quietly. He arrived during a particularly bad cold spell, when the ice pulled limbs off trees, but we were all safe and I am grateful he is here, though he does not seem healthy.

There is something about him that worries me. I do not know what. His head is different. His eyes and his mouth seem too big for his face. My Pierre says he is fine, that I worry too much. When did he become such an expert in children?

Jean-Jean watches his brother and talks to him, points at things in the room, and tells him what they are. If the baby needs something, Jean-Jean will either fetch it for him, or come to me. Usually he comes for me, but when the baby needs his toy, Jean-Jean hands it to him, and often plays with him.

Little Paul is a sickly child. I do not know if he will live to go with us again. He takes the breast, but does not seem to want much, then becomes restless. No amount of bouncing or burping seems to help. And his face looks like that of an old man. He has big round eyes, an over-large mouth, and his ears, larger than usual, stick out from his head. I call him my Little Bird because if he learns to flap those ears, he will fly away from us.

Anna says he is fine, just fussy, that as he grows, his face will grow into its features. I wonder.

No. 20 - *Thunder Moon, 1809*

When the thunder rolls across the heavens, Paul jerks and his eyes go all big and round. A good boy, he does not cry, but I can tell it bothers him.

Jean-Jean loves the storms and holds Paul and tells him it is just the Thunder God rolling rocks across the clouds. He tells Paul it is but a game and not to be afraid. Paul's eyes just get bigger, and sometimes, if the storm is really close, Paul not only jerks his little body, but he shakes all over, like a frightened dog.

Paul walks now and follows Jean-Jean everywhere. At least they do not go off in different directions. But he doesn't talk. Anna says that is normal, that the older one knows what he is saying and tells us. She says he will talk soon enough, to enjoy the quiet while I have it.

As I learn more English, I notice Anna's voice softens. She will never be as quiet as an Indian—but I will never be as loud as the Americans.

There are children in Saint Louis, but Jean-Jean and Paul seem happy being by themselves. Perhaps it is the loudness of the American children? Paul does not care for loud noises of any kind.

No. 21 - *Falling Leaf Moon, 1809*

Jean-Jean is excited about the hunting trip. He has been promised his own bow and arrows. My Pierre said he would make them. Paul, of course, wants his own. I will make him one if my Pierre doesn't make two sets.

This will be a different hunt than usual. Papa Pierre has a job downriver and will not join us. My Pierre says he thinks it will be the last hunt of the Trappers Dorion. At least all together.

Paul still wants the breast, though not often. He also eats off Jean-Jean's plate. Jean-Jean is so patient with his brother. I wonder how it will be when we're on the hunt, and Jean-Jean wants to go with his father or uncles and not play with his little brother.

I hope Paul survives this winter. I have made fur hats

and coats for all of us. I hope they will be enough.

No. 22 - *Thunder Moon, 1810*

Anna was right. Little Paul does seem to be growing into his face, but he is still sickly. He seems to tire easily and never fusses when I put him down for a nap. If he is tired and I do not notice, he will crawl into his bed or curl under the table, and sleep.

The hunt this year was better than last year. Paul was happy to stay with me when Jean-Jean went off with his papa or uncles. I made Paul a little bow and some arrows, but he didn't seem too interested in them. He mostly sat with me or followed me around the campsite as I did my chores. Jean-Jean shot every tree and shrub he could find, until he lost all his arrows. He reused the ones he could find until they, too, were broken or lost.

Many times I woke in the night to see Paul staring into the dark, the light from the fire reflected in his big, round eyes. If he noticed me watching, he'd point. The next day, Pierre would take him and go look. There was always a track of some animal right where Paul pointed. Sometimes a deer, sometimes a wolf, often small animals. Jean-Jean was always jealous, as he wanted to see, too. And shoot it with one of his arrows.

Now that we are back in the cabin, Paul seems a bit less jittery. Even the thunder does not bother him as much as it did. He does not enjoy it like his brother does, but he is not as frightened of it.

Jean-Jean is still the patient big brother and takes Paul

with him everywhere he goes.

No. 23 - *Moon of the Long Night, 1810*

My Pierre spends more and more time in the saloons. He says that is where the men who need guides and interpreters come, and he must go where the jobs are. He has been hired by several men for a few weeks at a time, but it is winter now, and few people need or want a guide. Those who hunted went in the fall; those who trap are already gone. The cold is brought by winds from the north, and it chills one all the way through to their bones.

The boys are healthy. Or, at least, Jean-Jean is. I am still not sure about Paul. Anna continues to teach me English, and to assure me Paul will be fine and to stop worrying. Paul no longer wants my milk and eats solid foods. While Jean-Jean eats as much as I will give him, Paul needs to be coaxed, and even then, he eats but little.

Three nights ago, my Pierre came home drunk but with some money. I am not sure, but I think he said a man named Manuel Lisa got him drunk in order to get him to agree to guide and interpret for his party into Sioux country.

When he woke, he laughed and said he'd be back in a few days, but he would not work for Lisa, or any man who got him drunk and tricked him into signing a contract. Especially after he said he did not want to do it. When Lisa came to the cabin, I did not know where my Pierre was. Lisa demanded his money back. I had no idea what he talked about. I fear my Pierre plays a dangerous game.

I cannot convince my husband that his reputation is his

livelihood, and if he gets the reputation of a thief, no one will hire him. Wives, he tells me, are to be quiet and respectful and should not tell their husbands what they should or should not do.

PART II

JOURNEY
TO THE OREGON COUNTRY

1811–1812

No. 24 - *Cold Moon, 1811*

It is almost the Hunger Moon, and my Pierre has come out of hiding. The Spaniard, Manuel Lisa, has taken his party and gone upriver.

My Pierre spent all the money he was given for the job. Most was spent on the firewater, but some of it he spent on food for his family.

An American—M. Hunt—came to town and found my Pierre. Like Lisa, M. Hunt leads a party of men to hunt and trap the beaver. He wants to cross the Great Mountains, as did the expedition of Messrs. Lewis and Clark. He needs a guide, and he needs an interpreter who speaks Sioux. Unlike Lisa, M. Hunt did not get my Pierre drunk. He also promised my Pierre money but only gave him a little, and said the rest would come later. I think M. Hunt heard about what happened between my husband and Manuel Lisa.

My Pierre came home, showed me the money, and laughed. He said we would make money just by collecting the advances, and then he would hide until they no longer stayed in town and would go on without him. I am sure the white men have laws against that, and once word gets out, my Pierre will go to jail—or worse. Why can he not understand this is a dangerous thing he does? Papa Pierre would be very angry with him.

I became very angry and told my husband that he must honor this commitment. His temper rose, and he roared as he came toward me with his hand raised to strike me. It was not the first time he had drunk the firewater and hit me. I stepped aside. He lost his balance, hit the table, and fell to the floor. I told him the boys and I would go up the river to find and meet with this M. Hunt, and that *I* would honor his bargain, if M. Hunt would take us. I told him that, if M. Hunt did not hire me, the boys and I would go to the tipi of my mother and that, if he wanted us, he would know where to find us.

His face purpled with rage; my Pierre stood and again came toward me; this time his hand curled into a fist. Had he not learned, even by then, I would defend myself? I picked up a piece of firewood and hit him on the side of his head. He dropped to the floor as if he was dead, but I checked, and he still breathed. I had not hit him as hard as I feared. I then put the boys, who silently watched, into their winter furs, gathered the things we would need, and we began our walk upriver, along the bank, looking for M. Hunt and his boat.

No. 25 - *Wolf Moon, 1811*

We walked all night. It was a cold and dark and slow walk with only the weak light of the moon to guide us. We walked along the edge of the river, over frozen fields, through thickets and grass stubble. The lack of light made it hard not to stumble on roots and rocks. We each carried a walking stick, which helped us to remain upright.

The boys were quiet, though when we stopped at daylight, they wanted to know if I had killed their papa. I smiled and told them that I had only made him go to sleep for a while. They were relieved he only slept, but they, too, tire of his firewater temper.

I made a small shelter for the boys, and when Paul rolled up in his robe, he watched me with those big, round eyes of his, accusing me of something, but I do not know what. He said not a word, to his brother or to me. I began to wonder if his eyes would ever close in sleep.

Jean-Jean wanted to know if his papa would come for us, or if we would go back. He wanted to know if M. Hunt would take us. I told him if his papa did not come for us, we would go to the tipi of my mother to live, and he and Paul would have lots of friends to play with. I told him I did not know if M. Hunt would take me in place of their papa, but that I would ask. Jean-Jean then rolled next to his brother, and they both slept.

I will let them sleep a while, and then we will go on. I do not want my Pierre to find us before we find M. Hunt. I want to walk while there is light to see by. Then, when we camp again, the boys can sleep all night.

No. 26 - *Wolf Moon, 1811*

We did not have to go far before we came to M. Hunt's boats, anchored close to the shore. I carried Paul, asleep in his sling, but he wiggled his arm out and pointed toward the boats; then he pulled his arm back into the warmth and went back to sleep.

We went a short way beyond where the boats were anchored, and I made a low shelter where we could see but not be seen.

If my Pierre does not come soon, I will know he does

not want us, and I myself will approach M. Hunt to seek the job, or at least passage to my mother's village.

It is a waiting game, now. The boys play quietly, and we watch, and listen. We can hear the men on the boat, and see them through the grass, but they do not see us.

I understand most of what I hear. Anna did a good job teaching me English, though I still speak it with slowness and, she says, with a thick French accent. The boys speak English almost as well as they speak French. Anna says both languages are crib languages to them. I had never heard of a crib language, and when I told her, she smiled and explained it means the language the baby hears growing up.

Paul stopped playing and pointed in the direction from which we walked. Pierre had arrived. The boys wanted to run to him, but I motioned them to stay still and be quiet and listen.

Pierre called out to M. Hunt and asked where we were. M. Hunt told him he had not seen us and to get onboard, that they were ready to pull anchor. Pierre argued, but when Hunt sent the small boat, he finally went. His eyes searched the shoreline, looking for us, his family.

The boys watched but remained quiet. I could see the confusion on their faces. Why, they seemed to ask with their eyes, did I not go to their papa?

No. 27 - Warm Moon, 1811

As soon as my Pierre was on board Hunt's boat, I took the hands of the boys, and we walked to the water's edge and stood. Pierre espied us and asked M. Hunt to take us. I do not think he wanted to, but I could not hear him, as his back was to us. I could only hear my Pierre. They talked with much arm waving, and I heard my Pierre tell him if he would not take us that he would swim back to shore and not guide him. Angry and defeated, M. Hunt sent a boat for us.

I heard him tell my Pierre that if we got in the way, even once, he would put us ashore and leave us. I will make certain that we do not get in the way, and he will see that we will be most helpful.

It is now warm enough to write, and the boys are quietly playing their games. I found out from one of the men, a M. Reed, that M. Hunt told him he feared having a woman and two children on board would slow the party down but my Pierre assured him, and everyone, that we would be useful, and so we were allowed to come.

I think the men are now happy we came. I help with the cooking and make moccasins for the men. The boys stay out of their way, unless called by someone to help or go hunting. The men, if not busy, are generous with the boys. They tell the boys stories, and make them toys, and sometimes play with them. It is like the boys have many uncles.

Jean-Jean comes back from the hunts with wondrous tales. And the men marvel at how Paul seems to hear and accurately point to the game. Jean-Jean says Paul prefers hunting wild berries along the shore where he can keep an eye on me. I do not know how Jean-Jean knows what Paul says, but I remind them both that the wild berries are not yet ripe enough to eat. They say nothing in response to my admonition but smile at me as if they share a secret only they know. I watch, but neither seems to suffer from eating too many green berries, so I relax.

Many of the men are surprised I can write and that I keep a journal. Some of the men also keep journals, and a few of the voyageurs can read a little, too. I trade lessons with those who are interested. I learn more English and practice what I learn in return for teaching them to at least write their names.

No. 28 - 21 March 1811

It is nice to have the correct date. I like the moons and their names, but unless I count each day, calendars are more precise. Or at least that is what Father Lark said when he taught us to use one many years ago.

It was hard to sleep last night, as the frogs are out in full song. The rains still fall, but they seem warmer and softer. The trees along the river are covered in soft greens and pinks of soon-to-be leaves and flowers.

The boys were quietly playing when Paul stiffened and looked up on the nearest shore. He pointed, then turned and pointed to the far shore. It was then my Pierre met some of his old friends from the Osage and Ioway and the Potawatomie, Sioux, and Sawkee. They were feuding amongst themselves, and a huge war party of about 300 warriors milled along both banks of the river.

The men in the boats were nervous, not knowing who the braves were going to battle; but my boys were excited. They had never before seen a war party and wanted to join in. They did not care whose side they were on, they just wanted to fight. My Pierre talked to his friends and secured safe passage for us up the river, as we were not part of the feud. Once past the war party, the men began to relax, though they remained vigilant and kept their rifles close at hand.

We follow the Muddy and take the same trail that Messrs. Lewis and Clark took a few years ago.

I still think M. Hunt dislikes me, but he allowed me to see a page of his journal and seemed surprised I could read to him what he wrote. He writes his journal in French.

When I asked why, he said he hopes to publish it some day, and French is the language of the intelligent. I smiled at that, for I must be intelligent as my journal is also in French. He agreed to tell me the dates if I ask him. I shall try not to ask, at least not often, nor to let the boys pester him. He is a bit dour for such a young man.

No. 29 - April 1811

I would ask M. Reed the date, but he is still in Saint Joseph, taking care of business. He will catch up to us later.

The boys liked our time at Saint Joseph. Paul has taken to a young voyageur named Baptiste and follows him everywhere. The man is patient and often carries Paul on his shoulders. Because this Baptiste does not speak baby words to Paul, Paul learns to speak like an adult, though he is still more quiet than talkative, except when he is with his older brother.

It is good to see Paul not so quiet, though his eyes and his ears miss nothing, he smiles more, and asks more questions. And delights in pointing to things that Baptiste cannot see or hear but that often lead to game for dinner. Paul's ability to find game the others cannot see gets him invitations to go hunting from several of the men. My Pierre allows it, now and again.

At first, Jean-Jean was jealous of Paul's change of affection, but it is to his big brother that Paul comes at night and regales him with his stories of the day, so all is well between the brothers as they tell each other of their adventures.

I walk along the shore when it is easy to do so and gather leaves and barks and whatever seeds from last year I can find to use in cooking or in teas. The berries are not yet ripe enough to gather or to eat, but soon will be.

No. 30 - 8 April 1811

We will be here two days. I am glad for the stay. I think I am again with child, and there are women here whom I know. I would like to stay until our child is born. I tire of this traveling, especially carrying a child. I am sick in the morning and tired all day. It is hard to walk, let alone set up and take down our camps.

I would like another child, but is this the time? Perhaps it is just a touch of something and I am not pregnant. This trip will be hard enough without that.

Almost every night, when we are encamped, M. Hunt tells us how many miles we traveled. I have seen him take instruments out of boxes and look through them at the sun, but I do not know how they work. I asked M. Reed what they were called and how they worked. He told me that M. Hunt uses things called a chronometer and a sextant and sometimes an octant. He explained how they work, but if I cannot get close enough to see and touch, which I'm sure M. Hunt will never allow, I will never understand.

M. Reed laughed, and then said if he ever had the opportunity to show me, he would do so. I would love to know how the measurements are made and what one sees when one looks through instruments.

No. 31 - 11 April 1811

I told Pierre I am sick, that maybe I am with child, and asked if we could stay until the baby comes. I told him there were women here, friends; they would help. He yelled and told me we were on this trip because of me and that we would not stay. He picked up a stick and beat me.

He beat me in front of all the men. When he was through, he told me to get busy and pack our camp. That we were leaving and no one would wait for me.

Am I so selfish to want to have women about me when I have his baby that I deserve a beating? But he was right. It is my fault we are on this trip, and surely, when the baby comes, if I am with child, there will be other women to help.

The boys stayed very quiet. Paul watched his papa with wide, round eyes—the same accusatory look he had for me when we left Pierre in the cabin so long ago. He and Jean-Jean stayed close to each other all day, and watched their papa and me, and said little except to each other. Our little camp was very quiet. Paul did not even go with Baptiste.

Last night, Pierre asked me why I was so quiet. I said nothing and ignored him. I set up camp, made supper, and sat by myself. I know he had to prove he was a man and could keep his woman under control, but I do not have to like it. I said nothing. There will be no apology, from either of us, but such is married life.

No. 32 - 14 April 1811

With the winds favoring us and filling the sails, we have made good time and the men have not had to work so hard. I was told that many of the men went on ahead of us to wait for us at the Nodaway station, that soon our numbers will swell. A few of the men, including Paul's friend Baptiste, have gone to the Nodaway to tell the men of our eminent arrival. Paul feels abandoned by the sudden departure.

I am still sorry that I could not stay at Fort Osage but am happy to be on this journey. I remember the words of Father Lark. It seems he may have been right; I will go places and see things and do things I never thought of or imagined.

And it is good to see my husband without the firewater in his gut.

He has not apologized for beating me, and he should not, but last night he held me close in his arms as we slept and told me he loves me. I am forgiven. I told him I loved him, and he squeezed me a little tighter.

M. Hunt said he would stay on his present course and follow the same route that Lewis and Clark did a few years earlier, at least as far as the villages of the Arikara. Once at the villages, he will decide whether to continue on, or go south and west through the Dakotas, and cross Wyoming to the Snake River. He thought it might be faster going overland until we reach the Snake River.

The men talked quietly. That was unknown territory, and they were not sure they wanted to go that way. The voyageurs preferred the rivers and boats and canoes.

No. 33 - 17 April 1811

The river is swollen, fast, and filled with many drowned buffalo that float down the river. They are covered with turkey buzzards that feast on the bloating bodies. It is funny to watch as they fight among themselves for a particular place. There is enough for all, and then some. In death, the buffalo wear noisy and feathered headdresses.

Jean-Jean wanted to shoot the turkey buzzards with his arrows but feared he would not get them back. The boys think it great fun to watch the drowned animals float down the river. I am just grateful it is not any of our party! And that Jean-Jean does not shoot his arrows at the birds—or the buffalo. What a mess that would make if he shot a bloated buffalo.

We have reached the station near the Nodaway River where the main party waited for us. We are now more than 60 people, including the boys and myself. It appears most of the men waited here for us.

As long as there is a fire and warmth out of the rain where the boys can dry off when they tire of their play, they are happy. Paul again chases and goes to his friend Baptiste, who absented the party some time before to come ahead to the Nodaway encampment. Paul seems over his affront at being earlier abandoned by his friend.

The rains have not let up for days. It is warming, the snows in the mountains melt, and the rivers are swollen. I do not want the boys near the edge of the banks, as the fast waters undercut the edges and cause them to collapse without warning.

Now I am sure I am with child. I am sick in the morning

and tired all day. I have said nothing more to Pierre about it. He will figure it out in his own time. I harbor a secret dream that we will stay with the Arikara when we arrive at their villages. I will not speak of it, but I hope.

No. 34 - 22 April 1811

The snakes are out, warming themselves in the sunshine. Clouds of pigeons darken the sky; if they are on the ground eating, it looks like a snow storm blew in, the ground is so white. They are so numerous they break the branches of the trees on which they roost, much to the delight of the boys. The birds act like they have not eaten all winter. Anything they can find quickly disappears down their throats.

This morning M. Bradbury was not paying attention where he walked and was nearly bitten by a rattlesnake. By good chance, he heard it in time to stop and was far enough away to remain safe.

The men have tired of their usual fare, and as pigeon is good to eat, we have many pigeons to add to our pot. I have collected leaves of the spice bush, which gives a nice flavor to the stews. Some of the men prefer to clean their pigeons, stuff them with wild onions and spice bush leaves, and roast them on a stick over the fire, or maybe just toss them into the fire. Either way is good. However cooked, they are a welcome change.

At last, we are again on our way.

The boys and I walk along the river collecting various bulbs and greens to add to the cook pot. We are careful to stay away from the edge. The men on the boats warn us if there is a particularly bad place, where the bank has been undercut.

No. 35 - *28 April 1811*

There are signs of war parties, and we are all nervous. We see their fires at night, not too far away, so know they watch us. My Pierre has forbidden the boys and me to walk the banks in search of food. The men, he says, can do without fresh greens and onions.

The boys are excited, and watch the banks for any signs of war parties. At one point, Paul pointed to the far bank. By good fortune, it was not a warrior, only a deer coming to the river for a drink.

Every time he points, those who see him look toward where he points. Paul's reputation as a person able to hear what others cannot is well known and respected among the men.

When I ask him what he hears, he just looks at me with his round eyes and says he hears ghost-talk and will say no more.

He has not pointed to the war parties. Perhaps the ghost-talk tells him they mean us no harm. Or, perhaps, he knows that we know the warriors are out there and watch us, and he figures we can take care of ourselves without his help.

No. 36 - *30 April 1811*

The boys are disappointed. They expected the creek to be filled with colorful butterflies; instead, it is filled with water. They were excited to know we would come here, and now they feel cheated. They wanted to wade through the butterflies.

This is the last place we can find the trees of ash that are so well-suited to making the poles and oars that we need to get our boats farther up the river. The boys go with the men and help when called. Otherwise, they stay close but out of the way.

I use this time to jerk as much as I can of the meat the men bring and pack it for our trip. It is a time to gather what I can of herbs and wild onions to add to our food supply.

Jean-Jean helps find the trees and Paul listens. I often forget he is only two and a half years old. He points to game, but mostly he listens for the quiet steps of a man or war party. At least that is what I think.

Tribal children are taught to be quiet, but Paul's quiet is almost unnatural. It is as if he hears the winds speak words only he can hear and understand.

When he talks, it is barely loud enough to hear, as if he does not want to disturb the voices of nature, or the ghosts who speak to him.

I am feeling better, not as sick nor as tired, and the trip is actually interesting. I am glad, now, that we came, that my Pierre did not agree to stay at Fort Osage as I wanted.

I smile when I think of what Anna will say when we return and I tell her of my musings about Paul. She will laugh and tell me I have a great imagination. She will tell me that Paul is just Paul, and to stop trying to make him into a medicine man or a shaman.

No. 37 - 2 May 1811

Two of our hunters announced they would leave today. They said the trip was too long, and they wanted to return home. Pierre tried to buy their rifles, but they refused to sell either the rifles or their ammunition. They feared they would need both on the return trip, especially if they met any war parties.

The men were good hunters and brought us much game. Their absence will be hard for us. They departed with new moccasins and vests, which my Pierre said I could make but should not put any beadwork on as they had refused to sell him their rifles or ammunition. The men did pay me, with extra meat.

Paul told me after they were gone that one would make it home, the other would not. When I asked how he knew, he just looked at me with his eyes big and round as an owl's as it stares into the dark night searching for food. Sometimes I wonder who is the parent, who is the child?

What else does this boy-man son of mine know? I do not ask. I am not sure I want to know.

The rains have returned, and the river, where it had been shrinking, now swells again. And fast. We do not walk the river's edge but stay in the boats and, when possible, harvest the wild cress that grows in the river. It adds a nice peppery flavor to our food.

No. 38 - 8 May 1811

It was dark, and people were beginning to settle for the

night when Paul sat, then stood, and then pointed. Some of the men grabbed their guns and looked into the dark but discerned nothing. Paul did not move. A couple of the braver men actually walked into the woods but came back without having seen or heard anything. They smiled at Paul and told him it must have been an animal. Paul pointed again, and this time eleven naked Sioux warriors charged our camp, yelling and whooping. Jean-Jean grabbed his bow and arrows and stepped in front of Paul and me, but our men quickly had the invaders surrounded, with several rifles pointed directly at their hearts.

Surprised by our quick response, the warriors quickly changed their demeanor and placed their weapons on the ground. Pierre talked to them, and they told us they had been unsuccessful in war and were trying to appease the Great Spirit for the disgrace of having lost their battle.

In accordance with their beliefs, they had burned all their clothes and promised to devote their lives to the Great Spirit. Any unsuspecting white man they met would die to help appease their loss. Because of Paul's warning and our previous encounters with the Sioux, we were prepared, and no one died.

Jean-Jean was disappointed. He wanted to fight. He does not understand what pain and death a fight may bring. Paul walked straight to their leader and stared him down. The man backed up, visibly shaken by my son, who was brave enough to walk up to, and stare down, a war chief. When the man turned and walked away, Paul returned to my side and smiled. Whatever game he played, he won.

No. 39 - 10 May 1811

M. Hunt uses his timepiece and sextant at least twice a day and has informed us we have come about 800 miles.

When we reached the Omaha village, Hunt asked my Pierre why there were so few lodges and was told about the small pox which swept across the prairies in 1802 killing two out of every three people. Of those who survived, the older people are deeply scarred, but the children are free of it and their skin is beautiful and smooth. I fear the pox, but both my Pierre and M. Hunt assure me it has long gone, and we are safe.

M. Hunt said we would stay a few days, rest, and replenish our stores before going on. The boys eagerly look forward to playing with the children of the village. Well, Jean-Jean does. Paul is harder to understand. His eyes are large as he looks at all the lodges. He pulled Jean-Jean aside, pointed to one, and said, "No." He will not say more. And he will not go near anyone from that lodge. Neither does Jean-Jean. Neither do I.

I will enjoy having women near and perhaps trading some of my moccasins and vests for some of their beads and dyed bones, quills, and feathers.

My Pierre and I set up our camp away from the others, as we usually do, so we can have a little privacy and talk without being overheard. Of course, our talk ofttimes leads to the quiet and love conversations married folks share. Those talks are the best.

The sickness has passed, and I am no longer so tired. Having other women about to visit and trade with helps, too. While M. Hunt trades for meat and information, I trade for herbs and beads, and language lessons. Of course, I do not become fluent in the language, but I am able to speak a little. Between the words I learn, and the signing, I can carry on a conversation. I notice M. Hunt often looks at me as I talk with the women. He must use an interpreter, one of the men, or rely strictly on gestures.

No. 40 - 15 May 1811

Three men deserted while we were in the village, but two more joined us, even knowing we may have to fight the Sioux when we go farther upriver.

We were in a quiet part of the river, and the men were quiet and watched the banks—both for game and for war parties. Paul pointed up the river, toward a bend. The men quietly pulled their rifles closer to them. Two men in a canoe came around the bend to find several rifles pointed at them. They were white men, Messrs. Jones and Carson, and hired on to go with us.

We now head into Sioux country and then, M. Hunt says, to the Grand Tetons. Because there may be war parties on either bank, Hunt and the men confine the hunt for game to the islands in the middle of the river. The two new men are very experienced hunters who know this part of the country, and the Sioux, very well.

Everyone keeps his eyes on the banks to watch for enemy warriors. And I see many men turn, rather slyly, as if they are shamed to do so, to see if Paul points anywhere. If the men see me watching them, they smile and turn away, looking like they have been caught with their hand in the honey tree.

I sit, out of the way, and decorate moccasins for my Pierre and the boys. The women of the Omaha had many bright-colored beads to trade for my moccasins. The men look at my Pierre with admiration, as he wears such beautiful clothing. Some have come to ask that I make them clothes if they will bring me hides. I tell them to talk to Pierre, and he sets the price.

Jean-Jean keeps telling Paul to hear a war party. He wants to fight and prove himself a warrior. Paul smiles at his older brother but does not hear what is not there.

Did I make the right choice when I insisted we come? I keep my fears to myself and let the boys take what enjoyment they can find from this journey of adventure.

No. 41 - 26 May 1811

As we headed upriver today, Paul suddenly stood and pointed in the direction we traveled. One of the men observed him and quietly spoke to his partner. Everyone quickly grabbed their rifles and stopped talking. Soon, three white men in a canoe came into view.

Like the earlier men, they were surprised to see us and to have so many rifles trained on them. They said they were going home to Kentucky. M. Hunt told them where we were going, and they decided they were not ready to go home just yet. They joined our party. Each has his own rifle and ammunition and knows how to use them. Hunters are always welcome.

One of the new men asked how we had known they

were coming. Someone pointed to Paul and told them of his amazing ears. He said if Paul points, the men would do well to pay attention, as he not only points to enemies, but also he points to dinner, if they are fast enough with their rifles.

The men did not believe Paul could hear them, as they were quiet, but were assured that he did. Paul just stared at them—a wide-eyed child. A small boy wise beyond his years in ways I, his mother, will never fully understand. He must have told his friend Baptiste something, because I heard him tell the newcomers that Paul can hear the ghosts talk and they tell him things they tell no one else.

No. 42 - 31 May 11

Because we are in Sioux territory and have been warned they are not happy about it, the men, if they talk at all, speak softly. Their guns are close, and they check with frequency to see where Paul is looking.

Paul, with a peaceful face and relaxed body, stopped playing with his toy, looked up, and pointed to the far bank. When my Pierre looked, he saw a group of Sioux warriors. He and M. Hunt have crossed the river to talk to them and find out what they want. Once he knew his papa had seen them, Paul went back to his toy without concern.

Jean-Jean was very excited. He had his bow and quiver of arrows. The men were tense and serious, and checked their guns often to make sure they were ready if needed. Paul slowly turned, looking first across the river, and then up and down our side. He stopped, every time, and pointed first to one side of the Sioux and then to the other slowly moving his hand in a short arc.

Not for the first time, I wonder why I insisted on coming, and bringing the children. Adventure is one thing, putting my children in danger is something else. But, as my Pierre says, death is part of life, and we all will die at some time, unknown to us.

I sit and write as the boat gently rocks in the middle of the river.

It is later, now, and the men have returned. It seems the Sioux made motions of peace. They spread buffalo hides on the ground, built a fire, and offered the pipe of peace, which our men accepted and returned. M. Hunt spoke to the Sioux, and my Pierre translated.

Hunt told them we did not want their furs, but desired only to continue on across the mountains to the great Columbia River. He assured them we were peaceful and gave them presents of tobacco and corn.

The Chief said they did not want supplies or ammunition to go to their enemies, the Arikara, the Mandan, or the Minataree. M. Hunt assured them we would not supply their enemies with weapons or food or anything else to make the lives of their enemies easier.

Later, Pierre told me Hunt acted with correctness and showed no fear at all. That was good, for had he shown fear, we would have had to fight. The men were ready to fight. Jean-Jean was ready to fight. I was not.

Jean-Jean showed his disappointment, but when his father said a war party of over 600 warriors waited out of sight, he calmed down somewhat. My Pierre assured him he would get his chance to prove he was a mighty warrior, but he hoped not until he had become a man grown. Jean-Jean puffed his chest and said he was a man now. Pierre laughed, swung him up, and carried him around the camp on his shoulders.

When Paul heard how many warriors waited out of sight and that his father pointed in the same arc he had pointed, he smiled, then settled next to me. He found some sort of happiness in just knowing he had been correct.

No. 43 - 1 June 1811

We reached the Great Bend of the Missouri River. It nearly doubles back on itself, and the boys think it great fun that we float 30 miles on the river in order to travel what we could portage in a thousand feet of walking. Had we portaged, we would have carried goods and boats that distance, making several trips. We will, when finished, have gained very little, but it is easier to go upriver than portage everything across the land.

Jean-Jean wanted to walk across the land and meet the boats when we arrived, but Pierre, and the voyageurs dissuaded him of that notion. So did his younger brother.

Paul went into what I now call his alert stance. He pointed to the shore, but when a couple of the men went to see, there was nothing. Paul pointed again and then turned back to what he was doing. It made the men nervous, but they told each other it was merely an unseen deer. Surely, one said, had it been an enemy, Paul would not have shrugged his shoulders and returned to his toys.

No. 44 - 2 June 1811

We were still eating this morning when Paul stood and pointed in the same direction he pointed yesterday when nothing was there. This time his posture was different—he was stiff, not moving and barely breathing. The men, already nervous, made sure their rifles were ready and close at hand as they finished eating and prepared to pack.

Paul again pointed. Two chiefs stood on a high bank and waved their buffalo robes to show their peaceful intentions.

We immediately went to shore to see what they wanted. Jean-Jean stood in front of Paul and me with his bow and arrows, ready to protect us. We were not allowed on shore.

It seems the chiefs had earlier met two of our men, Messrs. Crooks and McLellan. At that time, it was not a peaceful meeting, and our two men escaped downriver. Now, the two chiefs ran to them to embrace them as if they were good friends, not sworn enemies.

Paul again pointed, this time across the river where a war tribe of about 300 Arikara, Mandan, and Minataree was gathered on the opposite shore. But at the shaking of hands between Messrs. Hunt, Crooks, McLellan, and the chiefs, all their hostility seemed to vanish like morning fog in the noonday sun.

The war party threw their weapons on the ground and swam to our boats, where they crowded on board to shake our hands in the white man's show of peace. Our men were not sure about their sudden friends and remained wary and on guard.

Paul watched everyone but stood relaxed, enjoying what he saw. *When did I become so dependent on him? When did the men?*

It seems the chiefs had abandoned their war plans, for now, in the hope of obtaining arms and ammunition from us. I breathed a sigh of relief when they absented themselves from our company. We continued along the river until we found a convenient island, pitched our tents, and set about making camp. M. Hunt said we would camp on the islands, out of Indian territory, as often as possible.

The chiefs and their men camped about a hundred yards away from us. There was much feasting between the two camps, and the warriors entertained us with dances and songs until late into the night.

One of the chiefs came over to Paul and stood in front of him for a long time. Then he reached down and touched him lightly on top of his head, removed his war tomahawk from his belt, and presented it to my little son.

This one, he said to whoever would listen, *is touched by the Great Wakan Tanka and will come to no harm.* I listened. And found comfort in the knowledge no harm would come to him.

Paul, true to form, said nothing but smiled his "thank you" for the tomahawk, which is almost as long as he is tall and almost too heavy for him to lift, let alone carry. He asked me to hold it for him and went to bed with a bigger than usual smile on his face.

No. 45 - 3 June 1811

The men are tired but strong. Many times they must go on the shore to pull the boats upriver using ropes, because the water is too shallow in places. They never complain, or at least, I never hear them. When they pull the boats, the hunters often go with them to act as guards.

Sometimes the boys and I are allowed to walk with them, and Jean-Jean often helps the men for a while, pulling the rope. He brags about how much he did until Paul looks at him. Then he grins, turns his hands palms up, and walks away.

Melons are ripening, and pawpaws. We have berries now, as well as greens.

The warriors have all gone, but two of the chiefs returned, asking for goods. M. Hunt gave them a few presents to show our good will, and the chiefs said more boats were coming up the river. As one, everyone turned to look first at Paul, then the river. Paul grinned.

While M. Hunt and the chief parlayed, Paul stiffened, turned, and pointed downstream. The men grabbed their rifles. It did not take long before the boats of Manuel Lisa appeared. We were all surprised, as Lisa's party left Saint Louis before we did. They must have gone up a side river to gather supplies and wait for better weather. M. Hunt told our men he did not want Lisa to get in front of us, as he wanted to reach the Arikara first. He and Lisa talked and agreed to each take a side of the river. Again, M. Hunt told our men that, no matter what happens on the river, they need to keep us in front of Lisa's party.

Lisa brought news that the Blackfeet have joined the

Sioux to keep fur traders out of their territories. For now at least we travel together, each to our own side of the river. There is safety in numbers.

Whenever Lisa looks over to see my Pierre or the boys and me, he glowers at us, especially at my Pierre. I am sure Lisa thinks my Pierre should be with him instead of Charbonneau. He also glowers at me, too. He probably thinks I was complicit in my Pierre's deceit. But he does not glare at Paul. It is obvious that Paul makes him nervous. And every time he looks at Jean-Jean, my son holds his bow up in a threatening manner. Once Jean-Jean even nocked an arrow as if he was going to shoot. Lisa is learning, I hope, to keep his dark looks focused elsewhere.

So we travel together for safety reasons, yet neither side trusts the other. And our brave and strong men keep us, always, in the lead.

Months before, when Lisa could not find my Pierre, he hired Toussaint Charbonneau and his wife, Sacajawea, to act as guides and interpreters. She, too, has a child, a son named Jean Baptiste. He is, she says, about the same age as Jean-Jean, but she left him in Saint Louis with the red-haired William Clark to be raised and educated by Clark and the Jesuits.

It was hard, she says, to leave him with Clark, but he will get a good education and be able to live and work with the white men better. She calls him Pomp, the name William Clark gave him, I think, and smiles when she talks about him. She misses him, she says, and enjoys the company of my boys. We joke that it is a good thing he did not come on the trip, because the boys, being the same age and having the same name, might get mixed up and go with the wrong mother.

She agrees with me the French have no imagination when it comes to naming their children — or their wives.

Jean-Jean told her she should have brought her Baptiste so they could become good friends and play and hunt together.

I wonder where Lisa and his party were all this time. They left before we did and should have been far ahead of us, not coming up behind.

No. 46 - *7 June 1811*

For three days we traveled in each other's company. The men from both camps went hunting together and shared the meat equally. And then Lisa let his anger out and caused trouble.

He found my Pierre and reminded him of his deception and the resulting debt. This made my Pierre very angry, as he thought then, and still believes, that Lisa deliberately made him drunk to trick him into signing the contract. He and Lisa began a loud and violent quarrel.

My Pierre went to M. Hunt's tent to tell him what Lisa had done, and then Lisa strode in telling M. Hunt he wished to borrow some towing line. I think he wanted to hear what my Pierre said.

Finding Pierre there, he berated my husband, who curled his fist and hit Lisa in the face. Lisa ran to his boat for a weapon with which to kill my Pierre. My Pierre then snatched up a set of pistols from M. Hunt's table and rushed out to kill Lisa.

There was much yelling from everyone, and people

came from both camps to see what was going on, and to defend their own champion. Much betting went on as to who would be buried and who would continue.

Lisa came at my Pierre with a knife. Messrs. Crooks and McLellan liked Pierre and thought Manuel Lisa a coward, so they were eager to champion my husband. There was more yelling and name calling, and finally M. Hunt pushed his way in, calmed people down a little, and stopped a general melee and possible bloodshed.

But Lisa, not ready to accept peace, made an insult to M. Hunt that could not be ignored. Angered, M. Hunt now became eager to join the fight and challenged Lisa to a duel. I kept the boys back as much as possible—not that I thought they should not see, but that I saw no need to put them in harm's way, even accidentally. Dueling pistols are not very accurate.

Lisa agreed to the duel, and went to his boat to get his pistols. Messrs. Bradbury and Breckenridge, the two naturalists who travel with us, followed him and, with much talk, managed to convince first Lisa and then M. Hunt not to duel.

Bloodshed averted, the two camps separated in anger. I doubt we will be sharing hunts or anything else with Lisa's men. It is probably the end of my friendship and visits with Sacajawea, at least for now. Perhaps, when we reach the Arikara villages, we can resume our friendship.

My Pierre was still so angry last night when we went to bed, he shook. But he is safe. At least for now. My boys still have a father, and I still have a husband.

No. 47 - 10 June 1811

Three Arikara came downriver today by canoe. Paul paid them no attention, so it was a surprise to suddenly find them in front of us. They informed my Pierre and M. Hunt that a war party wanted to stop us from passing through their lands, but the Arikara talked them out of attacking and have promised us safe passage to their three villages.

My Pierre is not sure he entirely believes them. He has forbidden the boys and me to walk along the shore without an armed escort. M. Hunt does not want to provide the escort, so we are confined to the boats. Jean-Jean says he will protect us, and Paul says he will listen extra hard, but Pierre says we are worth more than the strawberries, onions, and greens we might find for the cook pot.

As the day progressed, and it became hot, some of our men went ashore to hunt. They flushed a few birds and a sleeping buck from his nest in the grass. Prairie dogs, squirrels, and rabbits are plentiful, as are beaver. Several of the men returned with strawberries for the boys, as well as greens and a few roots for our dinner.

After the three Arikara men left in their canoe, the only humans we saw were the angry and sullen men of Lisa's party. Everyone is edgy—the men of Lisa's party must be as wary of us as we are of them. It seems to me we need to combine forces to face a common enemy, but I am only a woman; who listens to me? I am not even allowed to visit with Sacajawea. Men can be so childish.

No. 48 - 11 June 1811

The villagers live in dome-shaped stick lodges covered with mud. I see people sitting on top of these lodges, where they enjoy the sunshine as they work. The men make bows, the women shell beans or sew. They grow corn, pumpkins, and beans as well as tobacco and melons in large fields near their villages.

Of us all, Paul seems the most unconcerned. Still, I do not let either him or Jean-Jean go into the village, unless they are with my Pierre or me.

Paul gave his war tomahawk to me to carry and insists I wear it on my belt at all times. Women do not usually carry war tomahawks, but no one questions me, though some of the Arikara look at me askance. Conversations are quiet in both camps, as if each listens to hear what the others say. Paul ignores everyone from either camp.

Jean-Jean struts around our campsite with his bow and quiver of arrows. He assures his papa he will keep Paul and me safe. My Pierre has gone to M. Hunt's tent. A man came from Lisa's camp to talk to M. Hunt and decide how the two parties will enter the village tomorrow to meet with the Arikara.

I am glad Father Lark taught me to read and write and gave me this little journal. I hope, when we get to Fort Astoria, I can find another one. I hope I do not fill all of the pages before we arrive at that fabled place. He will be surprised and, I hope, pleased when we return and I show him my journal and tell of our adventures.

No. 49 - 12 June 1811

The boys and I stayed in our camp. It was a welcome day for the boys to run and play, and for me to tend to things that could not be done on the boat. We went hunting for berries and greens. Paul stopped, tapped Jean-Jean's arm, and then pointed. Jean-Jean grinned, raised his bow, and shot a rabbit. I showed him how to skin it, and clean it, and he did everything, and then presented me with the hide to tan. He placed the innards far from camp for other animals to find.

He is very proud that he has contributed meat to the cooking pot, and rightly so. My Pierre, too, will be happy for him when he returns from his hunt.

I caught some catfish for dinner tonight. My Pierre is not so fond of catfish; he says it tastes like river mud, but the boys and I like it.

A woman, Flowers of the Prairie, came to our camp and brought some berries for the boys. She has an easy smile, and I think we will become friends. Father Lark was right. I am meeting many people and learning new languages and ways of doing things. The sad part of all that is having to leave just as I make a new friend.

Of course, I do not speak the new language with fluency, but enough words are similar that, with signing, we can converse, with many giggles and with much laughter. The men also use me as interpreter when no one else is around.

No. 50 - 15 June 1811

As expected, my Pierre was very proud of Jean-Jean's prowess with the bow. He took him into one of the villages and helped him acquire a larger, heavier bow, with more arrows. The warrior he bargained with showed Jean-Jean how to make his own arrows, so he will not run out.

Jean-Jean offered his old bow to Paul, but Paul did not want it. It was a nice gesture, but the bow, even though small, is still too large for Paul. Jean-Jean gave it to the man to give to another boy to use.

There is much excitement in the village and the camp as the Cheyenne are coming to visit. The alarm raised earlier has proved false: the visit is friendly, not a war party. They travel with their women and children and even their elders.

We will be here for a while, as M. Hunt and Lisa have again become friends, and Lisa has sold many horses he keeps at a Mandan village to M. Hunt. Lisa, M. Hunt, and a couple of men have gone to collect them. My Pierre has also gone, taking Jean-Jean. Paul and I have remained at the camp, near the villages.

It did not take the villagers long to notice Paul is different from other children. If he points, they look. If he goes stiff and points, it is an enemy; if he is relaxed and points, it means either game or a friend.

The Arikara medicine man asked if he could adopt Paul and train him. His disappointment at my refusal was noticeable. I did say Paul could visit while we were encamped near the village, which pleased Paul and caused the man to smile.

Paul and the old man spend many hours together, and Paul is learning a little of the language though he does not talk about what he learned. With one barely two and a half years old, I wonder that either of them can carry on a true conversation, but they seem to enjoy each other's company, and that is important.

I did ask the old man if he knew what Paul heard when he pointed. He just smiled and said Paul heard the Great Spirit but would say no more to me about it, only that I have a very special boy.

No. 51 - 9 July 1811

We are still encamped near the Arikara. I feel like I have many husbands to cook and sew for, but none of the men have suggested anything else, for which I am grateful. I do still carry Paul's tomahawk, which brings some odd looks; as soon as Paul touches it, the people understand. But, then, women do not normally travel with such a large group of men. My Pierre is still out with M. Hunt, and I have no man for protection though I think the voyageurs would protect Paul and me if needed.

Today, Paul stiffened and pointed. Shortly after, a large war party began to come toward the village. The Arikara recognized the party as one of theirs, and people ran to meet the returning warriors. There was much yelling and wailing as women searched for and found their men—or did not.

Two of the main chiefs held a young man, badly wounded, between them. The chiefs said he proved himself with honor in battle. They brought him to the lodge of the medicine man. The mother of the young man ran to her son's side and held him in her arms as he died.

The mother is a widow and now has no man to care for her and her young children. One of the chiefs said he would take her into his lodge and raise her other sons and daughters as his, so she will be taken care of and her children will not want.

A feast was held for the returning warriors and in honor of the young man who died. There was much merriment, which Paul and I shared. At one point, Paul went to the side of the mother whose son just died. He said nothing, just stared at her and put his little hand on her arm. When she smiled at him, he nodded, then walked away. The mother wore the smile for several minutes before she entered her tipi.

I have made many moccasins and vests and leggings for the men and boys, and a new dress for myself. My new dress is open on the sides, held with laces, so when my belly is bigger, it can be opened. It has no sleeves, like a vest, and I can wear it over shirts if I get too cold. My leggings are also laced in the front to I can open them as the baby grows.

The baby is wiggling. I can feel it now and then, like a small tadpole in my stomach.

I am eager for my husband to return and eager for our journey to begin again so it can end. I hope we are in this place called Fort Astoria before the baby is born. I do not want her born on the journey.

No. 52 - 15 July 1811

The two naturalists are going home. Before they got into their canoe, M. Bradbury came to me and gave me his little inkpot and a quill pen. He has seen me writing and was very impressed. He told me almost the same thing Father Lark did, that I should maintain a record as I would meet many new people and see many new things. He gave me a waterproof pouch to keep my journal and pen in.

My Pierre, who returned with the other men and the horses three days ago, gave them each a pair of moccasins and a decorated vest I made for them. He again thanked them for the warning about Lisa's charge against him and for their help in getting that matter settled without either violence or jail time.

Jean-Jean and Paul gave each of them a feather to wear in their hair with the admonition to always wear it down, so people would know they were peaceful men. They laughed and gave each boy a hug and said how much they enjoyed knowing them.

As they went downriver, Paul looked at them, smiled, and waved.

It was not until they were far downriver I realized the inkpot had been filled with good ink, and not the ink I have been making from juice and soot. This gift, like my journal, is a treasure I will keep with me forever, no matter the hardships I may endure.

No. 53 - 18 July 1811

Our group is now 62 people, including the boys and me. M. Hunt bought 82 horses from Lisa and the Arikara. We now have enough horses to allow for 40 pack animals and for every two men to share one horse, so everyone can ride part of the time. My Pierre insisted I be given a horse to share with the boys.

At the moment, I find it more comfortable to walk than ride, so Jean-Jean and Paul often ride while I walk beside them.

The Arikara held a feast for us last night, with much food and dancing. The medicine man let Paul beat his drum, much to Paul's enjoyment. He then gave Paul a gourd rattle, and Paul shook it. The rattle is painted with black and red and yellow designs and has a leather thong wrapped and tied around its neck to make holding it easier. There is a loop large enough to go over his head so he does not have to carry it all the time. When Paul tired of shaking it, the old man placed the loop over Paul's head so he could wear it around his neck. On our return, Paul will be recognized and welcomed.

Some of Jean-Jean's young friends gave him arrows for his new bow, so his quiver is now full, and he has extras. My Pierre showed him how to roll them in a hide and tie it so they won't get lost.

Flowers of the Prairie gave me a pocket of tanned white deer hide. It is very soft. She was fascinated, watching me write in my journal, and made the pocket to fit over the pouch M. Bradbury gave me. She also gave me beadwork, some of the most beautiful I have ever seen, and a packet with some of her beads. There is room in the pocket not only for my journal pouch but also for the small packets of beads.

Lisa's party took their boats and departed this morning, going their own way. I will not miss them. I do not trust Lisa, and I am glad he is gone. But I will miss Sacajawea. As long as we were at the Arikara villages, we still visited and gossiped, often at the lodge of Flowers of the Prairie.

Lisa and his men will go up the Muddy. We will follow the Big River, for a while at least, and search for the Columbia River by going overland.

It is good to start what I hope is the last of our journey. I hope to be at Fort Astoria when the daughter of my Pierre Dorion is born.

No. 54 - 20 July 1811

We are encamped, having made small progress, as M. Crooks is sick and travels on a travois until he is better. Paul has gone to him, touched him, and shaken his rattle all around him in perfect imitation of the medicine man. M. Crooks assures Paul he will soon be well, thanks to his ministrations and caring.

As soon as Paul finished his dance and chant, in no language any of us understood, he stiffened and pointed. All eyes turned as a lone white man walked into camp.

He introduced himself as M. Rose and told M. Hunt he had lived with the Crow, knew them well, and would like to go with us on our journey. Hunt allowed him to join the party. The next day, several Crow rode into camp. When their eyes came to M. Rose, they threatened war over him if he was not sent away immediately, as they claimed he was a liar, a thief, and an evil man.

Paul walked to the Crow chief, stood by his side, pointed at M. Rose, and said the same thing. The chief looked down at Paul, and his medicine gourd, smiled, and said something I did not hear. Paul smiled back. Did he understand what the chief said? Or did he just respond to the smile and tone of voice?

Against the advice of his guides and several of the partners, M. Hunt has decided to keep Rose, at least for a time. Our men are not happy with the new addition and Rose stays away from Paul. But he did come to me, when my Pierre was gone. He wanted me to cook for him, to make him moccasins, to keep his bed warm at night. I told him if he came near me again, he would die. I reached down and touched Paul's war tomahawk. M. Rose followed my hand with his eyes and stepped away.

The prairie is all grass, with flowers. The grass is not so high here as in our long-grass prairies at home, where, unless one is on horseback, in many places one cannot see. There is also dust, much dust, which the horses and the men who walk kick into the air.

Although beautiful, the long-grass prairie is also frightening. If our boys got lost there, we might never find them. If a fire started, we could not outrun it. But here we are not in the long grass, and I am not too worried.

I have made and use a travois, which holds our equipment and camp supplies. Sometimes I walk beside the horse with Paul riding, and sometimes I ride holding Paul in the sling. We stay in the back of the column and keep M. Crooks company.

When M. Crooks no longer needs his travois, I will probably have to leave mine as they slow us down. But they make life so much easier. Paul likes to ride ours and talk to the ever-patient M. Crooks.

No. 55 - 24 July 1811

We are encamped along the banks of the Big River. We arrived yesterday, and as buffalo are plenty, Hunt says we will stay a fortnight. This will give us time to gather provisions, dry the meat, and make jerky, as well as give the invalids time to gather their health

Ben Jones, John Day, and some other hunters came upon a camp of Cheyenne. It turned out they were the same ones we met at the Arikara villages, so the men were able to acquire a few more horses and more meat.

I have noticed none of our men shirk from heavy work, but somehow the French seem more joyful than the Americans when they work. Perhaps it is their singing. The Americans seem more willing to offer help to me if they think I need it, though they are careful to ask my Pierre first, to make sure he will not be angered by their attentions.

Both the French and the Americans seem to enjoy the boys, so long as the boys do not pester or get in their way. Sometimes they will take Jean-Jean hunting with them. They tried teaching him to fire a rifle, but he prefers the bow, as it is lighter and easier for him to hold and shoot. They also like to take Paul, as he almost always finds game if it is to be found.

Away from the river, there are no trees. The grass is short, and the sagebrush is plentiful. It is too bad we are not like the horses. They can eat the sagebrush. It is hot, and the only thing that makes the heat bearable is the now-and-then breeze. I like the smell of the sage, when I can smell it. Being at the back of the line, mostly all I smell is dust.

No. 56 - 24 July 1811

Several of the men are sick, and M. Hunt told us we would stay here until the men got better. I have been making teas for them, but nothing seems to help.

Paul sings for each man and each man smiles and tells

him his singing helps to make them better.

The Cheyenne are staying with us, for a while at least. It is good company for everyone. Especially the boys and me.

If not for the cottonwoods by the river, the hills would be barren, with no shade. The grass is dry and brown and turns to dust when walked on. It even smells hot, as if Grandmother Earth has turned into a huge mud-brick oven and bakes everything that grows or walks upon her.

No. 57 - 6 August 1811

I am told these are not big hills, but they are the biggest I have seen. The men laugh, and tell me to wait until we are in the mountains!

All of the men have recovered from their illness except M. Crooks. He is better but still very weak and rides on the travois. M. Hunt has ordered us to continue up the Big River and hope we avoid the Sioux war party. Paul sometimes walks next to M. Crooks for a short ways, chanting and shaking his gourd. As slow as the horse walks as it pulls the travois, it is still too fast for Paul to keep up for long.

We follow the Big River and hope to avoid the Sioux who are on the warpath. M. Crooks is still on the travois, and Paul sometimes walks a short way with him, chanting and shaking his gourd. Slow as the horse walks pulling the travois, it is still too fast for Paul to keep up for long.

When we make our camp, the boys often go with the men to collect buffalo chips for our fires. There are no trees on the prairie to burn so we use prairie wood — the dried chips of the buffalo—to make our cooking fires.

My Pierre has gone with Messrs. Carson and Gardpie on a hunting trip. No one is concerned, as they are assumed to be trailing buffalo. Because we, too, are on the move, we leave signal fires for them—small, smoky fires that give off a thin column of smoke by day and larger blazing fires at night. Of course, if our men can see the fires, the Sioux can, too.

Paul listens, hears nothing, then shrugs his shoulders and goes on about his play. M. Rose is still with us, but if he moves anywhere near the boys, or me, one of the other men usually steps between us. I think he now understands that he is to leave us alone, but with my Pierre gone, I wonder how long he will behave himself....

Paul's friend, Big Baptiste, as Paul calls him, often walks with us, and when we camp, he sets his bedroll between the boys and me and M. Rose's. All the men quietly watch M. Rose, especially when he is anywhere near the boys or me. It is nice to know they will guard us and defend us if need be.

No. 58 - 8 August 1811

The men and I are getting worried. They agree that my Pierre and the others have become lost in these hills without even a tree for a marker. They climbed the highest hill near us and built a huge fire at the top and will keep it burning all night so it can be seen from a great distance.

Before we forsook our campsite in the morning, we added wet grass to the fire so the smoke would be seen for miles. The men tell me it is not uncommon for hunters to get lost out here where there are no unusual features to use as landmarks. The country looks the same, no matter which way you look—gentle, rolling hills covered in rocks and grass. No trees at all, no distinguishing shapes. I begin to worry about my Pierre.

This journey has become harder and slower. We go through shallow creeks and walk on sharp rocks, and everyone worries about M. Rose. He is a man not to be trusted. He is so sullen, he makes my Pierre look like a laughing man.

Paul does not like M. Rose. He stiffens and points every time M. Rose comes close. This has upset M. Rose, who calls Paul a freak and has threatened him harm. I think he fears my son. The men have let M. Rose know it would not be wise to harm Paul. Nor would it be wise for Paul to meet with an accident. M. Rose glowers at everyone.

A group as large as ours is easily spotted by tribal hunters and scouts and quickly reported on, without our being any the wiser. If watchers are out there, and I am sure they are, they must be peaceful, as Paul has not said anything—or pointed. If the tribes can find us, why not my Pierre and the others? They are all hunters and trackers.

No. 59 - 10 August 1811

The slopes of the hills, or mountains, are covered with crags and slabs of white rock. M. Reed said it is limestone, and soft, as far as rock goes. These rock formations rise up from the valley floor. The men tell me they are called buttes.

We observed a small herd of big horn sheep but could not get close enough to kill any. M. Reed says that is too bad, as their meat would be a welcome change for our diet.

M. Hunt had us build a huge fire on the top of the highest hill where we made our camp. I am worried. I do not wish to become a widow now. What would happen to my boys and me? Would Hunt sell us to the next tribe? Would Rose claim us? Would one of the voyageurs take us? I mustn't think like this, though the uncertainty gnaws at my heart.

Paul says Papa will return, that I must not worry. Jean-Jean says he will protect us and keep us safe. I smile for my boys, but my heart is heavy.

No. 60 - *11 August 1811*

Tonight, M. Hunt admitted he is getting worried. The others allowed they, too, are worried.

No one looked at me when they said this except M. Rose. He has spent too much time with the Crow, and I could not read his face.

Paul said all would come back. The men smiled when he said this, but I could see their eyes. They humored Paul, but he is only a child.

I looked across the fire, and M. Rose stared back at me, with a smile I could not read. A shiver ran up my spine. Big Baptiste must have seen it, too. He moved closer to where the boys and I sat.

No. 61 - 12 August 1811

We crossed two tributaries of the Big River that flowed from the southwest to the northeast.

Several of the men collected stones found near one of the rivers; they call the stones putrefactions and use them as whetstones to sharpen their knives and axes. Two of them showed the boys what to look for, and they, too, collected some of the stones for themselves, their papa, and me.

Paul wants me to sharpen his tomahawk. Maybe it is a good idea, especially since our men are not yet back and M. Rose keeps watching me. Let him watch, as I sharpen the blade of Paul's tomahawk.

No. 62 - 13 August 1811

Something has changed in the last day or so. M. Rose is friendlier. Even Paul does not point when he walks by. One of the men told me M. Hunt had a talk with him and said, the next group of Crow we came to, he would leave M. Rose with them.

Paul rode with me a while and told me that his papa and the other men were all right. I do not know why I trust in the word of a child who is not yet three years of age, but I am comforted by his statement.

I hope we do not have thunderstorms. The air is heavy, the clouds are dark, and my man will not see the fires if it rains.

Thinking the men were still on our right, M. Hunt took us west. We crossed a river that was 300 feet wide, swift of current but shallow. The boys walked it, holding onto me, and laughed and splashed each other in great merriment. M. Rose came by me and apologized. He said he was sorry that we got off to a bad start and promised not to hurt my son. He said if my man does not come back, and if I would like, he will take me as his woman and raise the boys as his, when we get to the Crow village. I stared straight ahead and said nothing, but my hand went to my knife where it hangs on a thong around my neck. He left. What makes him think I would go with him? He would sell us as slaves, I am sure.

I have given much thought to what I will do if the men do not return. I will approach Messrs. Hunt, Crooks, and Reed, and ask to continue on with them. They have seen my worth. I interpret for them, I help with the cooking, and the men come to me with their injuries, though I truly do not know why. I am as good a guide as my Pierre. I will go on to this Fort Astoria with my sons and settle there.

I hope the men find us soon.

No. 63 - 14 August 1811

I was cooking supper when the men arrived. They were very tired and almost drained of energy. They had spent days trying to find our trail, and never once did they see any of the signal fires or smoke columns we so carefully made for them. Two days ago, they found our trail and followed it to us.

My husband was especially grateful for the hot meal that waited him. And the boys were thrilled their papa was once again with them. There were many hugs all around and much laughter at their return.

After the feast, the men were too tired to dance and only wanted to sleep. I, too, will sleep soundly for the first time since my Pierre left. M. Rose did not look too happy at their return, but he was gracious.

No. 64 - 16 August 1811

We have turned south and west and will soon follow the south fork of the Big River, at least for a while. We are going to go through what M. Hunt calls the Slim Buttes, and then, the men tell me, I will see real mountains. They say that, though it is hot down here, I should be getting warm clothing ready for the boys and me. The mountains are high, and the air will be cold.

The buttes are amazing! They are wide in one direction and slim in the other, and made of white and reddish rock that juts almost straight up from the ground. I wish I could stay and explore them. Some of the men climbed one and

said the view was incredible, but I cannot make the climb to see for myself. It is too bad our two naturalists went home; I think they would like these buttes very much and could tell me about them.

I walk most of the time and lead the horse. The boys run until they exhaust themselves, and then they ride, Paul in front, Jean-Jean in back. Paul often sleeps while Jean-Jean holds him. If Paul is too tired and Jean-Jean does not want to ride and hold him, I carry him in his sling either as I walk or ride.

Paul is still small for his age, but is getting too big for me to carry. He grows so slowly, compared to Jean-Jean, all but his head. It seems huge, already full-grown, on his tiny frame, like a skull without muscle or skin. Even his hair is thin, making his eyes appear even larger.

No. 65 - 17 August 1811

The men killed a big horn sheep today. The meat was very good—similar to that of the sheep we have at home. Beheld some black-tailed deer, but the men say they are not as good to eat as the red-tailed deer. Still, the big horn was a welcome change in our cook pot, and any deer, no matter the color of his tail, would be welcome.

The trail we make is hot and dusty. There are no trees, no shade. Every step kicks up dust. There is no water and no passage that we can see through these barren mountains.

We walk, paying little attention to anything but the person in front of us and where we put our feet.

No. 66 - 18 August 1811

We turned back to the broken countryside. Our hunters killed eight buffalo.

After we set up our camp several of us climbed a nearby peak with gentle slopes. From the top we could see mountains far away to the west. Some of them seemed to have snow on their peaks, or perhaps they are topped with white rock.

Someone told me they are the Big Horn Mountains, and we will cross them, and even more and higher mountains farther on — the Grand Tetons.

I begin to despair that we will reach Fort Astoria before the baby is born.

My Pierre has already named her. He will not tell me the name, or why he is sure the baby will be a girl. I think he just wants a daughter.

For some reason, he seems to think I can choose to make it be either a girl or a boy and has told me he wants a daughter and that I am to produce one. And then he laughs his loud and joyous laugh.

It is easier to walk in this broken land only because we can spread out and not have to eat so much dust. But all must be vigilant for snakes. The boys each have a stick to beat the ground in front of them; they know to stop and be still if they hear the rattle of warning. When a rattler is killed, the man keeps the rattles and the skin, while the meat goes into the cook pot. Rattlesnake meat is white, and mild-flavored, and much favored.

No. 67 - 19 August 1811

We are encamped next to a pond surrounded by gooseberry bushes. All the berries are ripe, and some are red and some yellow and even some of green ones are ripe. There are also some cherries. The boys and I, with the men who are not hunting, pick as much of the fruits as we can. They will be good to take with us for their water and good to cook with for their flavor.

Unfortunately, we are not the only ones who have found this place. There is clear and ample sign that bears frequent the area, though none seem to be here now. Still, every little breeze that ruffles the leaves gives me a start. Paul laughs at me, but I cannot help it. Bears are territorial, and mama bears are more vicious even than she-wolves. I keep a sharp eye out for my boys and a wary eye on every bush that moves.

Thunder roars far away. Paul calls it a Sky Bear and the lightning he calls the Sky Bear's spears. By good luck—or the Sky Bear's bad aim—the lightning spears are thrown far from our camp.

No. 68 - 20 August 1811

The nights have turned cold and disagreeable. Last night it froze, and the ice was as thick as a silver dollar when we rose this morning. This countryside is high and harsh, with hot days and cold nights. The boys do not seem to notice. To them it is nothing but a great adventure. They run during the day until exhausted and then sleep all night.

There are trees by the river, so we have wood for fires. I keep busy making warm leggings and shirts for my man and boys. My Pierre says he will try to shoot a couple of wolves for hats for the boys.

The men surround the camp fires, and many of them are making their own cold weather clothing.

No. 69 - *22 August 1811*

My Pierre found a trail made by Crow, and we now follow it. It leads west, the direction we want. We have run out of water and suffer greatly. Especially the boys. Food is scarce, and I worry about my baby.

It was hot during the day, and the storms avoided us.

We could see the rain falling at a distance but never once did it fall on us.

I worry the baby will suffer from my lack of drinking water and not having enough to eat.

M. McKenzie's beloved dog died from thirst and exhaustion today. If only he could have held out just a few hours more. Late this afternoon, we came upon a shallow river that flows north. I do not understand the white man's way of treating dogs like people. His dog did no work, and he would not allow us to eat it when it died, even though we hunger and dog is good meat.

We are camped tonight beside this river. My Pierre and M. Hunt agree, if it is not the Powder River, it is one of its branches. It is shallow and wide, and the men said they drank as much mud as water but they did not care because the mud was wet.

The clear sky means it will be cold again tonight.

No. 70 - 23 August 1811

We traversed more barren hills with dry gullies, great heat, and a treacherous trail. Snakes are frequent, and I make the boys ride on the horse with me.

There is no game to be seen anywhere we look.

Everyone is hot, tired, and thirsty. We came upon another branch of the Powder River. Again it is wide and shallow, but the water seems a little more clear. The men and the horses are very glad of the water. So am I. So is the baby—she now kicks again.

No. 71 - 25 August 1811

When we finished drinking our fill of water, we turned to a small herd of buffalo that grazed nearby. We killed five and had a good meal. We cooked as much meat as we could to take with us. It will not last long in this heat.

Baby must be happy, as she again kicks every time I stop moving. Restful sleep becomes more and more difficult because of her.

No. 72 - 31 August 1811

After days of thirst and the loss of one dog because of it, we have reached what we think is the main branch of the Powder River. We set up camp at the high point of the

shore. None of us knows how fast the river will rise if the threatened rains come. We do not wish to be caught in a flood, and clouds roll overhead. I can smell the rain. I only hope it falls on us and not far away.

Everyone seems to have picked up their spirits, and the hunters have gone out and returned with meat.

The boys and I found buffalo berries and gooseberries as well as greens along the river's edge, so tonight we had a good meal. We will sleep well, I am sure. At least everyone else will. My sleep is ever dependent on the baby's sleeping. She does not like it when I am still.

I hope my baby is all right. Pierre is still sure the baby will be a girl, as beautiful and strong, he says, as her mother. I just want her – or him – to be alive and healthy.

Thunderstorms roll down the valley toward us. I need to stop writing before the storm arrives and the rain smears my words.

No. 73 - 1 September 1811

M. Hunt spent the day with a group of Crow and managed to trade our horses for 121 well-fed and mountain-trained ones. These horses are fresh and not weakened by the heat and lack of water. And they are used to the mountains, which will be good for us, as we go into and across them.

Found and picked many currants, more gooseberries, and even a few late strawberries. The hunters shot elk and black-tailed deer.

I am proud of my boys. They never complain. Even when thirsty, they do not whine or moan or cry. They are good little warriors.

The Crow have left us. I am saddened, as I welcomed the company of their women. Many of our men are very weak and tired. I do not mind going slower, as it gives me a chance to look around more, though I am in a hurry to get to Fort Astoria. Sometimes I wish the baby would tire, at least at night, so I could get some sleep. I find myself dozing in the sun when riding the horse.

M. Rose knew some of the Crow and rode away with them. The men seem relieved he has gone and taken his sour demeanor with him.

No. 74 - *4 September 1811*

M. Rose has returned with a few of his friends. He assured us of our safety and explained we travel too slowly for them to remain with us and that is why they left.

My Pierre set a slow pace, and those men still too weak from a few days ago are allowed to straggle behind and catch up as they will.

Our travels are slow, but healing. The baby moves more and more, especially when I am still. She wants me to move all the time. Sometimes I can barely sleep or get any rest all night.

M. Hunt tried to get us over the Big Horn Mountains taking the trail he thought the Crow chief had drawn for him, but we had to turn back. When we came out of the canyon, M. Rose and four Crow waited. M. Rose said the chief sent him to guide us to the correct pass. He said once he got us there, he and his friends would leave us.

Perhaps I was wrong about him. He has of late been polite and, like now, helpful when needed. Still, I am most grateful and relieved my Pierre came back to me. I would choose the Big Baptiste before I would choose M. Rose.

No. 75 - *6 September 1811*

Met eight families of Snake and Flathead as we crossed the pass.

I rode at the back of the column, holding a sleeping Paul, and no one but me saw him raise his hand and point. How could he hear them? He said "Good," smiled, and went back to sleep.

We continued west, across the mountains, and dropped down onto the grasslands. I picked more berries and dug some bulbs as we walked. We beheld many elk and deer, and even some buffalo. My Pierre and some of the men went hunting.

No. 76 - *7 September 1811*

Again, game and water are scarce.

No. 77 - *9 September 1811*

These Shoshone and Flatheads are a large group, and their women and children travel with them. They are friendly, and my boys enjoy company their own age. Children seem to speak their own language. Perhaps they should become our interpreters.

For a few days, I had female companionship. The women taught me what they could of their language and showed me new beading designs. We traded beads and designs, and one of the women drew a design on a piece of leather and gave it to me. She told me to make something for the baby so the baby will know she is always welcome among the Shoshone.

I was able to trade with them for some tanned hides to

make shirts and vests to go with the new leggings and moccasins I have made for the boys and my Pierre and myself.

The men have brought in elk and black-tail deer. There are still strawberries to be found, though they are small and shriveled. But the flavor is good. I have smoked as much meat as we can carry and have made pemmican and packed it in the bags I made from the hides. I do not want to be hungry again. It is not good for the boys to be hungry, or the baby.

I saved the bladders of our game to carry water in case we need it once we leave the Big Horn River. I do not want to thirst again, ever!

We still travel too slowly. The tribes have moved on, and we now travel on our own to the Wind River.

Will we ever be out of these mountains? The days are still warm, but the nights are icy and cold.

It is nice to sleep curled against my man. Especially when his daughter lets me sleep.

No. 78 - 13 September 1811

The mountains have closed in and are rugged. The terrain is tortuous to ride or walk. The peaks are high, the winds strong and constant.

The walls of the canyon are almost straight up and a gorgeous red. I just wish they were friendlier to horses and people. The shore by the river is rocky and narrow. There are few trees and little game.

No. 79 - 15 September 1811

My Pierre and the men are grumbling tonight. M. Hunt said we should leave the river, which the men want to follow, and go back and take the Indian Road. My Pierre says they are making a big mistake to do this, but M. Hunt says he is the boss and will not listen to his guides.

The men lose faith in M. Hunt. They think he should have stayed in Saint Louis and remained a businessman if he will not listen to men who are more experienced than he is.

I am too tired to care. I am ready for this journey to end. I want only to reach Fort Astoria and have this baby.

No. 80 - 16 September 1811

We climbed a high pass but can see nothing as we have been in a cloud since we began. It is cold and wet, and the trail is muddy and slippery. M. Hunt assures us there is a valley below and that the Grand Teton Mountains are only about 100 miles away. Once across them, all waters, he says, flow to the Mighty Columbia.

O! I think we must be almost there. I will be in Fort Astoria when the baby is born. I am not the only one who is happy; the men have declared a feast and a dance this night.

The boys and I will stay at our campsite. It has been a long day of walking along what M. Hunt calls the Spanish River and the Shoshone call the Seeds-Kee-Dee Agie or Prairie Chicken River. The boys and I are very tired, and a day at camp will be appreciated while the men hunt. We will look for the prairie chickens in the hopes of catching some for dinner.

No. 81 - 17 September 1811

Buffalo are plentiful, and M. Hunt said we will camp here, at Horse Creek Meadows, for a few days to hunt and rest. Not only are the buffalo plentiful but beaver and otter abound, as well as ducks and geese, and berries. This is a land of plenty and will be hard to leave.

M. Hunt says we have crossed the Great Divide, and all rivers that flow west will flow to the Great Columbia. Or beyond, M. Hunt says, to the Pacific Ocean. It looks to me like the Prairie Chicken River flows south, but perhaps it bends later, and I just do not know.

We still have some mountains to cross, mainly the Grand Tetons. M. Hunt says the Snake River is on the other side of the Tetons, that it flows into the Columbia, and we should be able to canoe the rest of the way once we get there.

I asked M. Reed what an ocean was, and he said it was a huge, huge lake, so big you cannot see the opposite shore, only it has salt water in it, not fresh. He says I will see it when we get to Fort Astoria. Father Lark was right; I am seeing many wonders in my life. And I have many questions; such as, will we ever be out of mountains again?

How I wish Father Lark could be here. I also wish for a flat plain on which to walk, instead of staring at more mountains first to ascend and then to descend!

But we are close to the Snake River, and M. Hunt says we can canoe the rest of the way, and it should only be a matter of weeks before we arrive at Fort Astoria.

No. 82 - *18 September 1811*

M. Hunt, some of the men, the boys, and I followed a small creek that came out of the mountains and came across a group of Shoshone drying buffalo. They were very frightened of us, even though they could see the two boys and me. Paul called out in Shoshone, "Good." But they did not listen and ran.

We followed them and met them in their village, where we convinced them we meant no harm. M. Hunt managed to buy 2,000 pounds of buffalo meat, and beaver pelts and other furs.

Paul held them in thrall with his singing and dancing. Soon everyone laughed and joined in the merriment, their fears forgotten like last night's bad dreams.

M. Hunt hired two Shoshone to guide us through the Tetons.

No. 83 - 25 September 1811

Today we climbed a small mountain and came to a good trail leading, M. Hunt says, to a tributary of the Columbia where it flows from another mountain range. The trail goes through a small valley. There are trees on the hills, but the floor of the valley is a meadow, with a creek running through it.

Maybe the daughter of Pierre will be born in Fort Astoria after all!

After the valley, the trail again became steep and narrower. Also colder and icy under the snow that covers the ground. Parts of the trail are very slippery. I make Jean-Jean walk and use his stick, and I carry Paul.

A pack horse slipped and fell about 200 feet into the river but was uninjured and waited with calm patience as some men went to get her. I am so glad it was not my horse with my boys on it.

Trees here are thick and such a dark green they are almost black. It would be next to impossible to take a horse through the forest without a trail, the trees are so close to each other. And the trees have a strange scent. They do not smell sweet, like the cottonwood, but sharp though not unpleasant. They have needles that are short and sharp, and not welcoming to either man nor horse. I am grateful for both the trail and the guides as we climb this pass.

No. 84 - 1 October 1811

My Pierre told me the men told him this is really part of the Snake River, that they call it the Mad River because it crashes through the mountains in a very angry and mad manner.

The water coursing through the mountains is white and swift. Some of the men want to go down in canoes, especially the voyageurs. M. Hunt is inclined to agree; however, some of the men walked down the river for a way and came back to report we could not negotiate it in canoes. Instead, we will go to Henry's Post to build canoes and enter the river on the other side of the mountains, where it is not so mad.

I do not want to go down this river. I think it is called Mad River because anyone mad enough to ride it will die. I can say nothing. M. Hunt is in a hurry to get to Fort Astoria, and he says this river flows into the Columbia. I would rather go over the mountains than down this gushing part of the river. Jean-Jean is disappointed. He thinks he could do it, with help from the voyageurs.

Paul does not like it either, but now no one pays attention to him. Or to me. Even my Pierre is eager for this trip to end, and he, John Day, and M. Reed have gone farther down the Mad River to see if it becomes navigable in a short time.

Several of our trappers wintered over at Henry's Post two years ago. They say it is near Henry's Fork of the Snake River and that there are good trees for canoes. They also say the river there is broad and swift, but not mad. O wish M. Hunt would listen to his guides.

No. 85 - *2 October 1811*

My Pierre and the men have returned. They say it is too treacherous to go down. That settles it; we will go to Henry's Post. I do not care where we go, so long as I can get dry and warm. There are two cabins and a lean-to at Henry's Post, so at least we will be out of the weather. It is cold and there are snowflakes in the rain that comes down upon us.

No. 86 - *4 October 1811*

We are all cold and wet. Broke camp this morning and forded the Mad River. It was fast and freezing water up to the bellies of our horses. Our Shoshone guides led us over the mountains and down to a large valley. We are now encamped at the foot of the mountains on the western side. There is fresh water and game, and wood for a fire. I fear I shall never be warm again. We are about four days away from Henry's Post, the men tell us.

No. 87 - 8 October 1811

Today is cold. I am glad my Pierre insisted I make the warm clothes. The winds are from the west and bring flurries of snow. The deserted cabins offer shelter from the wind and the snow. The lean-to is gone, so there is no shelter for the horses.

The voyageurs are eager to begin building canoes and getting back to the water they know and love; they are already felling trees to hollow for dugouts.

Messrs. Hoback and Robinson and some others have decided to leave the company and go out on their own.

Robinson is a strange man. Though he had been scalped by enemies when younger, he holds no hatred for the man who did it. He will lead the group when they depart.

Jean-Jean has announced that he, too, will go with Messrs. Hoback and Robinson to learn to be a trapper. My Pierre spoke to him and promised that, when we reach Fort Astoria, he will take him trapping and he can earn his own money. Jean-Jean has decided to wait. I think M. Robinson helped convince him when he told Jean-Jean I would not be there to cook for them and Jean-Jean would have to eat whatever he himself could cook.

Paul has been even quieter than normal. He places his tomahawk on the floor and shakes his gourd over it. And points in the direction of the Mad River.

On our way here to Henry's Post, we followed a little river through a beautiful valley with many antelope and frozen and unripe cherries. For now we are out of the wind and weather. And we have a fire for a bit of warmth and cooking.

No. 88 - 10 October 1811

My belly grows, and the baby is only happy when I walk and move. When I sit to write, she kicks. When I lie with my Pierre, she kicks. I get no sleep and little rest. My fingers are too cold to hold the pen; I shall try to remember all that happens so I can write it when I am again warm enough to move my fingers.

No. 89 - 14 October 1811

A poor man of the Shuker or Digger tribe of Snakes came to the cabins today wanting something to eat. I had a pot on the stove and gave him a bowl of food, which he ate. He left after that. I do not recall that he spoke to anyone. My Pierre was not here, and the Snake seemed confused that a woman and two children were with all these men.

The creek next to Henry's Post is not very big, and the water seems to be going down daily, so the men are floating the logs and canoes to deeper water and then hauling them out to the bank to finish. We will have to walk a ways to get to the canoes when it is time to leave, but that is fine. It will be good to be in a canoe again and only weeks, perhaps days, from Fort Astoria.

No. 90 - 17 October 1811

M. Hunt told us to cache the rest of our unnecessaries tomorrow and be ready to leave the day after, on the 19th.

The poor man who came the other day came again, this time with his starving son. When we fed them, they were very grateful, and before leaving our company, they gathered the paws and entrails of the beaver we had skinned and eaten.

Our saddles and horse gear have been cached, and M. Hunt has shown the two Snake guides where. They have promised to care for our caches and all of our horses until someone comes to collect them later, as we will need them for our return trip to Saint Louis.

I wish I could sleep. I wish I could get warm. I hope the canoe will keep the baby rocked and happy and she will let me sleep, or at least get some rest as we travel. I have little hope of getting warm in the canoe, but at least I can sit and cover myself with a blanket.

No. 91 - 18 October 1811

The men have chopped down, shaped, and hollowed 15 cottonwood trees. It will be good to be back on the water and begin this last part of our journey. The voyageurs are eager to hold paddles in their hands instead of reins. Everything is cached, and what we are taking is down by the shore. The voyageurs are loading the canoes to be ready when we arise in the morning.

No. 92 - 19 October 1811

It was dark when we arose, dark and cold and snowing. The boys liked the snow. Some of the men enlisted the help of Jean-Jean to carry small loads to the canoes. Paul wanted to help, so he shook his gourd over all the canoes as he danced around them, blessing them for this journey. No one made him stop.

By the time we had all our supplies loaded and were in the water and underway, the voyageurs were singing the *Alouette* song. One of the voyageurs had made each boy a paddle. They joined in the singing and helped to paddle the canoe. They felt very important. And I appreciated the thoughtfulness of the man who made the paddles for the boys.

I, too, paddled. It felt good to move and stretch, and must have been enough to keep the baby happy, for she did not kick so much. Perhaps the rocking of the canoe on the water and the motion of my paddling was enough movement to soothe her. But she will wake tonight!

M. Hunt says we went about 30 miles before we stopped for the day. He is concerned the Snake River is going in the wrong direction, but I heard our Snake guides assure him the river will make a big bend farther on and take us where we want to go. Our guides assured him we have yet to reach the Snake, we are still on Henry's Fork. We will meet the Snake tomorrow.

No. 93 - 20 October 1811

The first 20 miles or so we rode a swift but good river, which joined the Snake, and then Paul turned pale and pointed the direction we were going. By the time we understood what he pointed at, we were in the fast waters. M. Reed tells me they are called rapids because they move so fast. I made the boys pull their paddles in and hold on. I feared they might cause more problems for the voyageurs if they tried to help. I, too, pulled my paddle back and left the paddling to the men.

Two canoes were caught and twisted by the current and capsized. We managed to pull the men to shore and out of the water, but all the cargo was lost.

We traveled another 20 miles for a total of about 40 miles before we encamped for the night.

The baby slept all day, and now that I want to sleep, she wants to play. I will be glad when we are at Fort Astoria and she is born. M. Hunt still tells us it is not far if we stay on the river.

No. 94 - 21 October 1811

The river narrows and the mountain walls come straight down in places. The men towed the canoes on lines from the shores, though that makes them hard to control, but it is easier than carrying them.

The boys and I walked beside the men and found many flat-leaved cactus that look like beaver tails with long spikes. Many still had their fruit, so we very carefully harvested some. One of the voyageurs told me they call them Prairie Figs.

The boys like going through the rapids. None of us likes the portages, but we like them better than going over the falls where we may die.

It is cold, but I do not feel the cold as much as the men. The baby helps keep me warm. And the boys run as much as they can when we are not in the canoes. They are very good about not getting in the way, and as soon as Paul tires, I carry him, with my pack, until we are back in the canoe.

We did not get far today. The men are getting frustrated. They are used to travel on rivers more gentle than this Snake. They, too, want this journey to end.

No. 95 - 23 Oct 1811

M. Hunt ordered us to lighten the canoes as much as possible to get through the rough waters. We went through several rapids, none of them dangerous, but all very swift. The boys enjoyed them and whooped with joy and begged for more.

Paul seems to have accepted the river, and no longer lets us know when rapids are ahead. His eyes remain round and watching, and he frequently reaches to me to touch his tomahawk and gourd, which I now carry so they will not be lost in the river.

He did point to several beaver lodges he spied near the shore, and lots of duck and geese. The men were almost too busy to look, but they did. After all, beaver is why we make this trip. They discussed where the beaver sign was seen, and each repeated it several times to get the markers in their memory.

Paul was delighted to see flights of robins and, especially, magpies. The black and white magpie feathers delighted him as they ran across the ground and then flew. It seems odd to see so many birds this late in the year.

M. Hunt says we are 75 miles closer to our goal. If it gets no rougher than this, we should be in Fort Astoria well before the daughter of Pierre arrives. That is welcome news, indeed.

No. 96 - 24 October 1811

M. Hunt says we have come almost 300 miles since seeing any other people. By the end of the day, the river widened and the current slowed. Paul pointed to the shore and we beheld several streams on either side, and then villages came into our sight. Smoke rose from their cooking fires, as well as delectable smells of cooking food. Suddenly, we all hungered.

When the people espied us, they fled, afraid. They must not have recognized I was a woman and had two children with me. Some of the men went ashore and tried to coax them back, to no avail. The men went into the village and found small fish about an inch long, along with roots and seeds, that were drying for winter, and cooking pots made of tightly woven grass. They found well-made fishnets hanging from the walls inside their tipis.

Paul wanted to go into the village to shake his rattle

and call them back, but he was ignored by everyone. He called out to tell them we came in peace and needed their help, but they would not hear him.

The men left some trinkets and two knives where they would be found and returned to the canoes. Farther downstream, we met some men on a reed raft. They wore no clothing, no leggings or shirts, only a bit of rabbit fur over their shoulders. Were they poor? Or did they not want to be weighed down if they fell into the river? They refused to come close enough so we could talk, so we continued on our journey.

My Pierre said their bows and arrows were well-made and beautifully decorated. He wished he could have held one to study it, for they looked like none he had ever seen.

We stopped that night near a waterfall about 30 feet high. Surely, this trip is almost over. Surely, the Columbia is close, and then it will be just a matter of days before we reach our destination.

I am cold and more than ready to stop this journeying. If I am cold, the men must be more so, but never have I heard them complain. Nor do the boys complain. Perhaps they do not realize they are cold?

No. 97 - 25 October 1811

We had a six-mile portage around some falls and rapids. The men again tried to lower some canoes into the river by rope but swamped them. No one was hurt, but many of our supplies were lost, including food and traps and rifles.

The river channel has become windy and narrow, and

the banks are again steep. M. Hunt says we only made 12 miles today because of the long portages.

The wind and the rain drive the cold clear through our clothes to our very bones. I can barely hold the quill to write, my fingers are so cold.

No. 98 - 26 October 1811

Today was a good day. We traveled about 70 miles, according to M. Hunt. Much of that distance was rapids but not treacherous. Paul napped much of the day; Jean-Jean paddled. He tells everyone he will be a voyageur when he becomes a man. The men smile. They remember, even if he does not, that not too long ago he was going to become a trapper.

We met more people today who ran away when they espied us. We did not try to call them back, just stayed on the river.

I am so tired! I hope I can get some sleep this night. Baby slept all day, so I have little hope. At least, curled against my Pierre, I should be able to get a little warmth.

No. 99 - 27 October 1811

We are all wet and cold. It rained all day; however, the river widened out after the rapids this morning and is beautiful. It runs swift and smooth, and the shores are far enough apart that we have no rapids to contend with.

M. Hunt told us we only made 40 miles, but I do not

care. Every mile brings me closer to Fort Astoria and the birth of this baby. If the rest of the river is like this, it will be easy and relatively fast. Dare I hope?

No. 100 - 28 October 1811

We passed through several more rapids and were not too worried. Then Paul stiffened and pointed. Before anyone noticed besides myself, the river narrowed into a tight gorge only 40 feet wide, and the first canoes shot through it before anyone could react. Below the gorge the water spun in what M. Reed called a whirlpool, and the canoe with Messrs. Crooks and Clappine hit a rock and broke. Poor M. Clappine! He was washed down the river and died before anyone could come to his aid. M. Crooks made it to shore and was saved. It was almost like the Mad River, only shorter.

We lost more merchandise and supplies, and the boys lost a friend. Paul shook his gourd and sang a song for M. Clappine. He is very sad his songs at the beginning of our journey were not strong enough to save our canoes and, especially, M. Clappine. I have tried to comfort him. I tell him his medicine is strong, but when the Great Spirit decides, his decision will be followed.

M. Hunt sent some men on the south bank farther downstream to reconnoiter and see if they would find more narrow gorges and whirling pools of water or if the river would again become navigable. He and some men walked the north bank.

What few of M. Clappine's possessions could be saved from the river were given to M. Crooks.

We went only 18 miles today.

No. 101 - 29 October 1811

M. Hunt and his men returned, very tired and frustrated. M. Hunt said they went about 35 miles, and the river twists and winds and is filled with rapids and falls. He said in some places the river falls are only 10 feet high while others appear to be about 30 feet high, not navigable for canoes.

The men who checked the south rim thought they found a place about six miles downriver, if we portage that far. Another long portage.

After we went to bed and the boys were asleep, my Pierre told me we only have food for about five days. He said the game is scarce, we have no horses to go hunting, and he is not sure what will happen to us.

I told him we would make it, and his daughter — for he still insists the baby will be his daughter — will be born in the now-fabled Fort Astoria of Oregon Country.

He held me close, and I slept a little before his daughter insisted I wake.

No. 102 - 31 October 1811

M. Reed and three other men went down the river today hoping to find some friendly Indians who would sell us horses and provisions. They also wanted to learn if it is worth continuing farther on the river.

Sixteen men took four of our canoes and tried to go downriver. Those of us who stayed started digging holes to cache all but our most important supplies that we would need with us. The rain fell so hard and so thick, we could not finish digging the caches. We could not get out of the rain while we worked, and all of us were wet to the skin.

My Pierre wanted me to stay with the boys under a small shelter he built us. I was able to keep a fire going, but the wood was too wet to burn well. Still, it helps that the men can warm themselves with the hot water to drink. I found and roasted some roots. The boys and I ate a few, but most of them went into the pot of hot water to add a bit of flavor and maybe a little nourishment.

The rain here is constant. Not like back home where it would rain, then go away. I think I will never get dry. Most of us are now huddled under our blankets, trying to stay warm, if not dry. I am so sorry I have nothing more to offer then men than the hot water with roots boiled in it.

No. 103 - 1 November 1811

The 16 men who departed yesterday with canoes lost one canoe and another load of cargo. The other canoes were caught in the rocks, but the cargo was saved. We can see no trees anywhere to make more canoes.

M. Hunt said he saw no way we could continue by water and called a meeting of the partners. When they finished their talk, they told the men the river is not navigable beyond where we are, and food is scarce. It was decided that, as smaller groups finding their own way, everyone had a better chance of survival, and we would all meet again in Fort Astoria, whenever and however everyone arrived.

M. McKenzie took four men and went north across the plains hoping to reach the Columbia. M. McClellan took three men downstream, while M. Crooks and three men went upriver. All search for food and friendly Indians.

My Pierre, the boys, and I remain with M. Hunt and 31 men. I think M. Crooks will try to go back to Henry's Post and get our horses. I hope he succeeds, that the horses are still there, waiting for him, but I imagine the horses are long gone by now.

No. 104 - 2 November 1811

We dug six more caches, took our four canoes, loaded them with necessaries, and paddled upstream to where we camped a few nights ago.

My Pierre does not like this waiting and wants a horse between his legs so he can hunt. Our food supplies dwindle, and I see my Pierre sharing his with Jean-Jean. I share mine with Paul.

I bring as much as I can find out on the prairie, but it is not much. Nothing we can eat seems to grow here. There is lots of sagebrush, which horses eat, but we are not horses; and we have no horses. We eat the flat-leafed cactus when I can build a fire to burn off the spikes and roast it.

No. 105 - 4 November 1811

This afternoon, Paul stood and pointed upriver, where we found M. Crooks and his men returned, unable to make it to Henry's Post. They found us where we had encamped on the 27th October.

We were a somber group, as we had already gone beyond hope that he would return with our horses and no longer expected him to do so.

The eight beaver he brought were welcome, though not enough for all of us to eat our fill, but enough so everyone had a bit of meat in their plate of soup.

My Pierre's temper began to flare; he never wanted to give up the horses and had argued against it, and now the group had no way to get close enough to game, should they find any, to kill it and bring it back. Pierre took Jean-Jean out to set traps, but naught came of them.

This constant cold and rain has all the men jittery. None of us wants to wait; we all want to go, to end this horrible trip. We are, all of us, cold, wet, hungry, and miserable, and we are perturbed at M. Hunt's lack of leadership. The men mutter he should have stayed in his office back east.

No. 106 - 5 November 1811

Jean-Jean tried to trap small animals, but they are underground for the winter and not interested in coming out. Besides, he had no decent bait to entice them.

Paul looks about with his big, round eyes. I cannot tell if

he is afraid or curious. He stays by my side, his hand on either the tomahawk in my belt or on the gourd he now wears all the time. He says nothing, just watches all about him, and us.

My Pierre goes alone onto the prairie searching for game but comes home empty-handed and ever more angry. He would be well-fed, if he could eat his anger.

No. 107 - 6 November 1811

M. Hunt set a net in the river and caught only one fish. Not enough for everyone, even when cooked in a stew. But it helped some.

Two of M. Reed's men returned to camp after exploring the south rim. They did not bring good news, nor did they bring food. I kept the boys with me while the men talked. I could hear my Pierre's voice now and then. No one sounded happy.

We cached all but the few essentials we still had, and those were divided into individual packs. Each of us carries about 20 pounds of food. The river has been deemed not suitable for canoes, and Messrs. Crooks and Hunt have decided to divide us into two groups to go our own way.

We will stay on the north bank with M. Hunt, while M. Crooks and his men will take the south shore, and we will all meet again once we reach Fort Astoria.

I look at my boys and wonder how long the men will be willing to share their food. Will my baby live? I am hungry all the time, I am tired, and Paul must be carried more and more, as he is hungry, tired, and weak.

No. 108 - 7 November 1811

My Pierre is very angry. We have lost nine days in this futile effort to find a way to safely navigate the river. The voyageurs mutter and agree with him. Even they would prefer a horse to having to walk on this rough and rocky plain. The plain does not even hold water to make mud on which to walk. It is thin dirt and sharp rocks.

Paul is very heavy, especially when added to the weight of my pack and the baby. If I fall behind, I will be abandoned, so I dare not slow or stop to rest.

Someone caught five beaver. We dried the meat as much as possible as it is better to eat when dry, but it is hard to do in this constant rain.

No. 109 - 8 November 1811

We stayed here another day, to cache even more. The remaining food has been divided for each man and myself. We will each carry our share of meat, corn, fat, and bouillon tablets.

We do not have much to keep us alive. I hope it is enough. My share must be divided. My Pierre shares a bit, but it is important he keep his strength as much as he can to hunt and talk with any people we meet.

The boys and I are always hungry. I am sure the baby is, too. She still kicks but not with as much vigor. I can now get a little rest, but I worry more about her.

I wonder if we will make it to Fort Astoria in time for the baby to be born. I wonder if we will live to reach Fort

Astoria. I wonder if I will ever again be dry, let alone warm.

I wish Father Lark was here to pray for us.

No. 110 - 9 November 1811

The rain that stayed away for the last couple of days returned this afternoon. The wind, cold enough by itself, is now colder because we all wear wet clothes and sleep in wet furs and blankets.

Twenty of us, plus the boys, follow the north bank of the river as much as we can. It is not easy to follow the bank, because the rim is often broken and the going too rough for anyone to walk.

When my Pierre is moving, his temper is damped a bit. All the men snap and snarl at the slightest provocation, yet they work together. Brothers in a family of need.

We are encamped under a rock overhang at the edge of the rim. We thirst, and the river is below, but it is nigh impossible to reach and dangerous to try, because the canyon walls are steep. At least we are out of the rain.

We set pots and hides out to catch the rain, but the wind blows the hides, and the rain comes at such an angle that it rarely goes into the pots. Many of the bladder canteens I made have long since gone into our soup pots.

We have found chokecherries along the walk. They help assuage our hunger, though not much.

M. Hunt said we walked about 11 miles.

No. 111 - 10 November 1811

It is hard to walk so close to the river and yet be unable to get any water other than what we can find in the hollows of a few rocks. The water drains underground as fast as it falls. We can see water falling down the side of the far canyon wall, but it comes from within the wall itself, starting about half way down. There are no creeks or rivers on top that we can see or gain access to. We sometimes see the same on our side of the rim.

The boys, like the rest of us, are hungry and thirsty, but

they do not complain. Jean-Jean walks with me; Paul naps in his sling. I hold him with my right arm, my pack with my left, and hope I do not stumble or fall.

At last we came to a place where we could reach the river. The water revived us all, and once again I heard laughter. We drank our fill, and filled whatever canteens we had. We had not saved many, because we did not think we would be walking in a desert.

Except for this one place, the banks are sheer rock, 200 to 300 feet high. There is no way to climb down them for water, let alone to climb back up.

We have turned and now head northwest. M. Hunt says we went about 30 miles. I wonder if we have, or if he says it trying to keep our spirits up.

Some of the men have boiled their old moccasins with chokecherries and whatever else they could find. Some added bits of the sagebrush to flavor the water. They say a little bit is a very strong flavorant.

Sometimes Pierre carries Jean-Jean on his shoulders. Paul does not like to ride on mine; he prefers the sling. I think he feels unsure on my shoulders, with nothing to hold onto but my hair and thus no way to nap. It also makes me feel more unbalanced and vulnerable to falling.

I no longer see anything in front of me but the back of whatever man I follow. My feet hurt, my body aches. I want to sleep, but if I stop, I will be deserted and left to die.

No. 112 - 11 November 1811

My Pierre found a well-traveled horse trail at the river's

edge, so we followed it. Paul woke in the sling and pointed in the direction we walked, never opening his eyes. He is so tired and hungry, and just dead weight. We encountered two Shoshone coming down the trail; they led us to their village of reed tipis. The village women were terrified and fled. Perhaps we look like Spirit Walkers? We are all so thin maybe they thought we were dead.

It was not until the Shoshone men took us into their lodge to feed us that we realized the women were in such a hurry to get away from us they did not take their children who were too young to walk. I espied some straw in the corner moving and walked over to see what it was. I uncovered and gazed upon a terrified child. I smiled, made soft noises, and tickled its stomach, and it smiled back at me. I placed the straw back on it to keep it warm and safe.

One of the Shoshone took us back to the river, lined by their tents, and showed us where to camp. We all felt remarkably better after filling our stomachs. These people are very kind and generous.

No sooner were we settled than about 50 men came to visit. Paul was not concerned, and we found the men to be honest and helpful. They told us the river was broken by rapids for a long way, and it would be difficult to go by canoe or raft.

No. 113 - 12 November 1811.

M. Hunt bought two dogs, one of which we ate for breakfast. The other went with us when we left. He will go in the stew pot later.

Jean-Jean walked today, having had a good rest and a full belly. Paul was more amenable to riding my shoulders, at least for a while. He did not want to ride his father's. I do not know why. I wish he would; my feet hurt and my hips ache.

No. 114 - *13 November 1811*

The boys are very brave little warriors. I know they are tired and hungry, but they neither cry nor complain.

More and more, Paul looks like an old man in a small body. He speaks even less than usual, and though he runs a little when we camp, his short legs cannot keep up with us, so I must still carry him. Though he is almost three, I now see the blessing of his small size.

I turned back a few pages and read earlier entries – did I really say I wanted a flat plain? This plain is flat, barren, cold, and wet, with nothing to make shelters of, and no food to gather.

I could almost wish for the mountains again. At least there we had wood for fires and shelters.

I tire of this trip. Of carrying a baby. Of carrying Paul. Tired, cold, and hungry, I long for the comfort of my own tipi, a fire, and women friends.

No. 115 - 14 November 1811

We came upon another camp today. I think they are Shoshone but am not sure. They are dressed poorly if at all. Many wear nothing, though a few wear at least a hide around their shoulders.

They have several drying racks set up, but all that is upon them are the skins and heads of the fish with little flesh. Obviously, they have cached the rest for winter and are not willing to share.

Perhaps M. Hunt, or my Pierre, can convince them that their help is needed or we all shall die.

It seems we walked a far distance, as we walked all day. M. Hunt said we walked about 22 miles before getting here and are now encamped near the Shoshone people.

Our group has broken into smaller groups of four or five men for cooking and eating. My Pierre and I have two men with us, as well as the boys. It is up to us to gather our own food, cook it, and divide it. I let my Pierre divide the food, so the men will not think I take more than my share.

No. 116 - 15 November 1811

Once the Shoshone determined our need, and that we were honest and would not steal from them, they sold us two dogs and some smoked salmon before we took our leave of them.

It is cold but not raining, and our spirits are much lifted by that fact. Ahead of us are snow-covered mountains. From here, it looks like the river runs right through them.

The banks of the river are littered with dead salmon. The Shoshone tell me they come upriver to lay their eggs and then die. It smells bad, but the dead fish feed bear, coyote, crows, and other scavengers. Jean-Jean likes to throw rocks at them. He wanted to shoot them with his bow and arrows but decided he did not want his arrows stinking of dead fish.

Before we made our camp, we met some men on horseback. They kept their horses away from us, afraid we would steal them, but they did give us some news. They said they had met some of our people a few days prior to our arrival.

We ate the salmon we got earlier for supper and will keep the dogs for later.

My Pierre thinks I am silly to keep writing, but I cannot sleep well, and it does not disturb anyone. Again, his daughter does not like me to rest. She is most insistent I move. All the time. I wish he could carry her a while in his belly and let me sleep all night, just for one night.

Did Father Lark see this trip in my future? Does he know the outcome? How I wish I could ask him. How I wish this trip would end soon, before the baby is born.

No. 117 - *16 November 1811*

Again, the river is inaccessible with steep sides of sheer rock. It is narrow and filled with rushing white water that is beautiful to watch but noisy, and deadly if one should fall into it. I do not let the boys near the edge of the bank for fear it might give way and they would fall in. We could never get them if that should happen. They would be lost forever.

We ate one of the dogs to break our fast. We cooked it in a stew and will take the other dog and some parched corn for a later meal. It is not much but will keep us alive. There are four adults in our meal group, and we divide the meal in four parts, with the boys and I sharing my portion.

If we do not get horses soon, and if the men do not kill some game soon, we will starve. Many times I ask myself why I was so stubborn and insistent that my Pierre and I come on this trip. I hope my stubbornness will not be the death of us all.

No. 118 - *17 November 1811*

We met men today riding horses, and M. Hunt wanted to buy one. They did not want to sell, so Pierre talked to them. They reluctantly agreed to sell one in exchange for a tin kettle. M. Hunt declared it would be a pack animal. At least we can now walk without carrying our packs.

The countryside is empty. It is empty of trees and even of the sagebrush. After walking about 35 miles we found a river and set our camp next to it.

No. 119 - *18 November 1811*

It is easier walking with the baggage on the horse. My Pierre told me our food is limited to a small piece of fat for each person and a quart of grain. If we do not get food soon, it will bode ill for us all.

My mother came to me last night. She stood next to me and smiled, then held her hand out as she faded into the dark. Was it her ghost? Has my mother died? Are we going to join her?

We camped by the Snake River, after walking for 30 miles. The river has again become wide and smooth, perfect for canoes, but of course, we have none. And we have no horses except for M. Hunt's. We have no canoes, no food, and little hope.

What a bleak and barren place this is. There is nothing to stop the winds or the rains. And the snow makes it worse, because then we cannot see where to step. We step on rocks that turn and should be avoided, on stickers that go through our moccasins. What might be harvested to eat is hidden, or frozen and cannot be used.

I think, now, I am sorry I asked for a flat plain on which to walk.

No. 120 - 19 November 1811

Two men came to our camp and sold two horses to M. Hunt. They said the river is no good for canoes and that we have to go overland, across the plains. We have forsaken the river and now travel overland.

M. Hunt rides one horse; the other two are for pack animals. My Pierre tried to get one of the horses for me to ride, but M. Hunt said I could continue to walk. The men grumble that Hunt rides instead of walking—or allowing me to ride. He is not well-liked. The men think Hunt should offer me the horse.

We took what water we could from the river, but it did not last long. Now there is no water to be found, and we all thirst. Our hunger, too, is strong and debilitating.

No. 121 - 20 November 1811

It rained all night, and we captured what we could of it. It is a good thing, as some of the voyageurs were so thirsty they began to drink their own urine.

Never has rain been so welcome, even with the cold. The boys stood in the rain with their heads tilted back and let it fall into their mouths. They only stopped because it went into their noses. It was a slow way to drink, but fun for them. It gladdens my heart they can find fun in our misery.

No. 122 - 21 November 1811

We could see a river ahead, lined with willow and cottonwood. The river flowed west, out of the mountains to the north. Maybe we can make more canoes?

When we came to a village, an old man approached M. Hunt and accused him of stealing his horse and demanded it back.

M. Hunt told him he bought the horse from someone else, but the old man was firm. Because he wanted to trade with the villagers, M. Hunt returned the horse and bought some fish and two dogs. At least we will have food tonight and tomorrow. I do not feel much sympathy for M. Hunt.

Pierre managed to buy me a horse, so I no longer have

to walk. The boys can ride with me though I often still carry Paul in the sling. At least I do not have his full weight to hold when I am on the horse. The baby is happy when I ride; she gets a gentle rocking.

The rains of yesterday have not stopped. I am too cold and wet to write any more.

No. 123 - *22 November 1811*

Paul, tied snuggly against my back, wormed his arm out from under the robe and pointed straight ahead. A few minutes later, we met a small tribe coming toward us. My Pierre talked to them, and all they could tell him is that we have a long way to go. But they could give us no help on how to go other than pointing in a vague direction.

M. Hunt bought more fish from them, as well as two more horses and seven dogs.

The men of the tribe were interested in Paul as he peeked from under the robe, but when they came close, he shook his rattle at them, and they backed off.

We traveled about 35 wet, cold, and miserable miles today. I think this might be pretty country in the summer, but in the winter it is ugly and as miserable as I am.

No. 124 - *24 Nov 1811*

M. Reed called the river the Boise; it was deep and came up to the bellies of the horses. Pierre put Jean-Jean on the horse with me, so we stayed dry. Most of the men had to wade. The current was strong, the water cold, and a few of the men lost their footing but regained it quickly, though they were then soaked through. We lost nothing but did see much beaver sign.

No. 125 - 25 November 1811

Came to another river, which flows from the east, with plenty of beaver sign farther up it. When we forded it, everyone but the boys and I got wet this time. M. Hunt's feet got wet, but those who walked were wet to their waist. No one has sympathy for M. Hunt and his water-filled moccasins.

We are all cold and wet, from the rain if not the river, and hungry. Paul sleeps tied against my back, giving me some welcome support and relief. My Pierre has taken to carrying Jean-Jean more and more, unless he puts him on the horse behind me. When he does that, I carry Paul in the sling and we tie Jean-Jean on so he can sleep and not fall. The horse keeps the baby quiet, but I cannot sleep, though I doze, especially when my Pierre leads the horse.

I think I would brave another beating and ask to stop at least until the baby comes, but there is nothing to build shelters from, nothing to eat, and it is better to continue in silence. And hope we soon come to a negotiable part of the river and find trees to build canoes for the rest of this never-ending journey.

No. 126 - 26 November 1811

We see the foothills below and in front of the snowy mountains. They are barren, no different from the flat of the plains, just hilly. Will we have to go through them, or along their base? No one knows. We just keep walking, eating whatever we can find along the way. It is now every man for himself. My Pierre shares with the boys and me.

My Pierre found some frozen desert figs and brought them to us. The boys shared one; I ate a whole one. I do not know how many he ate or shared with the others.

I am too cold, and too hungry, to write.

No. 127 - 27 November 1811

We came to a pass so narrow and tight I had to get off the horse to get through it. The horse barely made it. The pass was not just narrow; it was filled with cold water, which we had to wade through.

My Pierre carried my pack, and I carried Paul. Jean-Jean walked on his own, tightly holding my robe. All of us suffer, no one complains.

Today someone caught a beaver, and when we camped, after 33 miles, we cooked and ate it. M. Hunt ordered a horse killed, and we ate that, too. The beaver went into a stew. The horse was cut up; some went into a stew, some pieces were tossed into the fire and roasted.

Everyone has had meat tonight. The food helps both our moods and our outlook. It also helps warm us. When there is enough, we cook for everyone and eat together.

No. 128 - 28 November 1811

I thought Paul slept, but he suddenly stiffened and sat up. He pointed ahead of us, so we were on our guard. Soon, we entered a village of Shoshone, arriving just after they killed two colts for food. In the winter, horse and ground flax seed are their only food.

M. Hunt bought a bag of the seed and some horsemeat, but they refused to sell him, or anyone in our group, a horse. They told my Pierre we had only three more nights in the mountains and then six nights to reach the Great Falls of the Columbia.

Neither M. Hunt nor my Pierre believes them. They think the Shoshone just want us to get out of their territory because they fear we will steal their horses.

No. 129 - 29 November 1811

There was no safe footing on the riverbanks, so we unloaded the horses, carried everything we have, and climbed into the mountains. The going was hard and steep and I thought the mountains too high for the horses, but they managed to climb them.

I carried Paul and my pack. My Pierre carried Jean-Jean and his gear.

I am so tired. We are so tired. We all just want to sleep.

The baby is not as active as she has been. At least she

still moves. I no longer think she will be born in whatever comfort I may find in Fort Astoria.

No. 130 - 30 November 1811

The mountains have squeezed the river channel into a narrow gorge. The water races through it as if it, too, wants to reach the Columbia River as fast as possible. The mountains are covered with pine forests and snow, and I am reminded again of how different the smell is from the trees back home. I still do not know a word to describe the sharp scent.

The trail is covered with sharp rocks, many unseen under the snow, and the side is steep and straight to the river. If one fell, there would be nothing to grab onto. My Pierre will not carry Jean-Jean because if he falls, they would both fall. One of the men twisted his ankle but does not think it broke. He tied a rag around it, because he must keep going. My Pierre reminded the men to walk toe first and feel for their footing.

Paul pointed into the forest, and my Pierre followed the point. He slowly raised his rifle, aimed, and killed a black-tailed deer, so we will eat when we make our evening camp. No one complained about having to carry the extra weight.

We covered 28 miles, according to M. Hunt. I am surprised, considering the treacherousness of the trail.

No. 131 - 1 December 1811

I do not know which is more comfortable, riding or walking. I get wet and cold either way. It is good to be off my feet, but it hurts my hips to ride. I cannot get comfortable any way I try. My Pierre wants me to ride, he thinks it is safer for me and easier for me to hold Paul. He is right about holding Paul.

It rains when we are in the valleys and snows when we are in the mountains. At times, the snow is as high as a man's knee.

The boys and I collected many frozen black cherries. They were delicious. We ate some but saved most. M. Reed said the frost brought out the sugar and cut the tartness. We caught a beaver and cooked it with the cherries. The flavor was good, but more important, it was hot food.

The men are weak, and the cold takes what strength they have. We can at least build shelters from the sage boughs if we can get them cut, to help keep us warm. The boughs make beds so we do not have to sleep on the ground. I like the smell of the sage. It is nice to sleep on, and it smells nice when it burns. I also like to crush the leaves between my fingers for the perfume.

No. 132 - 2 December 1811

We are all weak, and M. Hunt felt it best to rest in camp for a day, again, without food. He killed another horse, which helped ease our hunger.

I understand the need to stay and rest, but I want to get

to Fort Astoria before this baby comes. I worry about her. I am hungry all the time, and cold. How will that affect her? I do not want to have her in the snow and mountains. When I eat she kicks; when I have no food, she barely wiggles.

When I sit or lay down, Paul shakes his rattle over me and chants his songs. Like the men, I tell him his ministrations make me feel better.

No. 133 - *3 December 1811*

We again travel along the Snake. The trail was so narrow we had to unpack the horses and carry everything. I carried Paul in the sling on my right hip, and our supplies in my left arm. Jean-Jean walked or rode his father's shoulders.

It took all day to go nine miles. I am exhausted. My Pierre is angry. He thinks M. Hunt should have stayed in the east or, at the least, listened to the men he hired to guide him. Many men grumble about M. Hunt. He is neither liked nor respected and is blamed for all our ills and our predicament. They wonder why he hired guides if he was not going to listen to them.

No. 134 - *4 December 1811*

The river again narrowed and we had to climb back into the mountains. They are now all about us. They are so steep I doubt the sun could find its way down here. If there is a sun. The clouds are so thick, I doubt the sun exists here.

The slopes are, in places, covered with pine trees and other evergreens, that add a bitter scent to the air. They give us something to sleep on and under at night. At least we do not have to sleep on the cold and wet ground.

We came upon a clearing in a patch of pine trees at sunset and built a great fire. That fire brought warmth and comfort and a bit of cheer, even though we only accomplished about four miles.

Everyone keeps watching Paul out of the corners of their eyes. Will he find us another deer? A beaver? A friendly tribe?

I think even the baby is cold; she does not move as much as she used to. Please, Little Lark, stay warm and healthy. Kick all you want, I shall survive. I just want you healthy when born. *Kick!*

No. 135 - 5 December 1811

We woke to a raging snowstorm. My Pierre said we were lucky to see 30 feet in front of us. We decided to get out of the mountains and back to the river if at all possible. At least there it should only be rain.

We ended up sliding down the mountainside to the river, which we could hear roaring but could not see for a long time. I could not maintain my balance and carry Paul; he had to hold on to my robe as best he could and walk on his own feet.

One of the horses fell several hundred feet, and we were all surprised when we got to the bottom to find him standing and waiting for us. He had not even lost his load!

If I had known he could have done so, I would have strapped Paul and myself onto him. The journey down would have been much faster.

The snow is only ankle deep here, and it is raining and a tiny bit warmer. At least I tell myself it is warmer.

We slaughtered another horse when we made camp, so we will all have meat tonight.

It is easier to write when I am not so hungry and when I am not so cold. And it gives me something to do when I cannot sleep because of the baby and her kicking.

No. 136 - 6 December 1811

We had just started out this morning when we noticed Paul excitedly pointing across the river. There stood M. Crooks and his men on the far shore, gesturing wildly. They appeared to be signaling for help. We made a canoe from the hide of the horse we killed last night and sent some food over to them.

One of M. Crooks's men, M. Prevost, refused to stay with his party and insisted on coming back with M. Delaunay. He got so excited at the prospect of eating that, mid-way across the river, he stood to dance and capsized the boat.

M. Delaunay was rescued, but M. Prevost was carried down the river and drowned. The boat was lost. They had gone six days with only their dogs to eat and were in worse condition than we were. M. Prevost should have known better; perhaps he was crazy from the hunger, but he put not only his life in jeopardy but that of M. Delaunay, too.

M. Crooks said that Messrs. Reed and McKenzie had passed them a few days ago and said that M. McClellan had forsaken the river to cross the mountains. He hoped to find the Flatheads and a shorter, faster way to Fort Astoria.

The river flows almost exactly east at this point. I fear it flows in a circle. And we will never reach the Columbia. I no longer think the Columbia River exists. I no longer think Fort Astoria exists.

No. 137 - *7 December 1811*

The loss of the horsehide boat yesterday was terrible. We no longer have a way to cross the river, and the men have set about building a raft out of whatever wood they can find. They have found enough, though it is not much.

M. Hunt crossed the river on the raft to talk with M. Crooks who is so weak he can barely follow his men, and then only with extreme difficulty. I do not think he ever recovered from his illness back at the Arikara villages.

That is all M. Hunt told us on his return.

Most of the men went ahead; my Pierre and I remained with those who stayed.

No. 138 - *8 December 1811*

The men made another raft to bring M. Crooks over, but he was too weak and ill to do it on his own. He had been dumped in the river before, and now the current was too swift, and he feared another dumping.

M. Hunt has decided we cannot stay with him or we will all die of starvation. M. Crooks is just too violently ill to travel. I am glad I do not have to make the decisions M. Hunt has to make.

I held my boys close as we settled in our camp. My Pierre will hold me close so I will get some warmth from him, and the boys will snuggle next to me on the other side. I am so tired I do not even hurt.

No. 139 - *9 December 1811*

Yesterday M. Hunt came back with one beaver skin. He said he left two with M. Crooks and the three men who stay with him. It was a thin soup for dinner. Everyone got a bite of the skin to chew and eat.

As we all waste from lack of food, Paul's eyes grow larger and larger. My wise little owl boy. Will he live to grow into his wisdom?

No. 140 - *10 December 1811*

I rode the horse, the only one we now have. M. Hunt wanted to kill it for food, but Pierre said no, it is mine. He had to lift me onto the horse as the baby has dropped. I feel like my bones are spreading, and I can barely walk. I cannot get comfortable, no matter how I move or sit.

We caught up with the advance party in the afternoon. They told my Pierre to shoot my horse, as they were starving, and again he refused. There were many grumbles, and some of the men made threatening motions, but Paul shook his rattle, and that seemed to quiet them. My Pierre said when we had to, he would, but not yet.

Not much later we entered a Shoshone village, and M. Hunt bought five horses. He immediately sent one back to M. Crooks and the men with him. They were able to put Crooks on the horse and catch up with us. In the meantime, M. Hunt slaughtered a horse, and we all ate. Some of the men had not eaten for three days. The men have forgotten their anger at my Pierre for not killing my horse.

This journey becomes tiresome. I long for Fort Astoria. I long for my own tipi. I long to be warm and dry, and I long for this baby to be born alive and healthy. I long to be among women.

No. 141 - 11 December 1811

Most of M. Crooks's men are on the other side of the river. One made a canoe and loaded it with his goods and tried to reach us. His canoe capsized, and he drowned. His goods were lost. They are not only cold and hungry, but all are demoralized and extremely weak.

M. Hunt ordered another horse killed, and he placed two horses with M. Crooks, as we deserted him and this place. We hope he can reach some friendly Indians farther upstream, but if we wait for M. Crooks to get better, we will all die.

Since the daughter of Pierre has dropped, I am more hungry than I have been since we began this journey to the Oregon Country. I think I could eat the whole horse and not share any of it.

No. 142 - 16 December 1811

Pierre and the men are unhappy; we have spent the last 20 days starving and wearing ourselves out and have gained nothing. We are back at our old campsite.

Paul pointed across the river, and there stood 13 freezing and starving men waving at us. They were one of the groups that had split from ours earlier. M. Hunt directed our men to build a canoe of horsehide, and eventually all the men and their possessions were brought across the river to join us.

Some Shoshone came to visit, and told us we cannot find a passage by following the river, that we will have to go overland. They pointed toward the mountains on the other side of the Snake. They said that beyond this point the river becomes very narrow and angry and is not possible to travel by canoe and there are no trails through the canyon.

I do not look forward to the cold of the snow. Or to climbing into those white barren mountains. Why can we not stay with the Shoshone? One look at my Pierre, and I know we cannot stay, and I know not to ask.

No. 143 - *17 December 1811*

We moved upstream a bit farther and made our camp near some Shoshone. They sold us a horse and a dog but did not seem to welcome our presence and watched us whenever we moved from our encampment, especially if we came near them.

Some of the women watched the boys and me, but when Jean-Jean and Paul started for the village and their boys, the women called their children to them.

Paul shook his rattle, and one of the elders came to him. He brought Paul a feather and put it in Paul's hair; then he patted his head, smiled, and left.

I look at their tipis with longing for the comfort of women and the warmth of the fire. But we are not welcome. I hope none of the women ever find themselves in my situation. The baby kicks and moves. I no longer walk, I waddle, and my bones no longer work properly. Neither of us is comfortable.

No. 144 - 18 December 1811

We needed a day of rest, which we had while M. Hunt and my Pierre spent the day with the Shoshone. They came back with another horse, some dried fish, and a few roots and dried cherries, pounded to a powder. It is similar to our pemmican, except there is no meat or fat in it.

Mostly, they got information about our route. The Shoshone said if we try to go now, we will die, that we should stay until warmer weather. They said the trail is good, but there is too much snow and too much cold.

M. Hunt tried to hire a guide, but no one would agree to take us until the snows leave. They said to travel now is to die, and they have families. They invited us to wait with them until the snows are gone. I looked at my Pierre, but he shook his head no.

Paul continued to point toward the mountains saying over and over to go, go.

No. 145 - 19 December 1811

I do not know if it was my Pierre or M. Hunt, but when they came back from the village today, they said one of the Shoshone has agreed to guide us over the mountains. He isss not excited to do so, but he agreed.

It seems the man who gave Paul the feather told the young man that we had a boy with us who has strong medicine, and he would keep us safe and alive.

Of course! I have been too close to my son to see it, but he is, or will become, a medicine man! It usually takes much training, and he is so young. I thought he was just being a boy, and somewhat humored by the other medicine men, but the Shoshone assured one and all Paul has strong medicine and will keep us all safe.

My hopes of staying and having women about me when the baby is born are dashed. I now hope only to be out of the mountains and the snow when she is born.

No. 146 - 21 December 1811

Paul's medicine is strong enough that two more Shoshone men agreed to help their friend guide us across the mountains through the snow and bitter cold.

Before we began crossing the Snake, the three guides came to Paul and blew sage smoke over him and themselves. Paul then sang a song and shook his rattle. Once their ceremony finished, the guides led us to the Snake River. Since we could not find any canoes, M. Hunt ordered two horses slaughtered and we used their hides to make boats.

The guides would not step into the canoes until Paul blessed them with a song, his rattle, and a dance. If they were not so serious it would have been funny—whoever heard of such a young medicine man? Yet, have we not, all of us, counted on him and his pointing for the whole trip? It has been in my heart that he knew the ways of the medicine man, but I have feared to even think the words, lest they anger the Great Spirit.

No. 147 - *23 December 1811*

It took one day to get all the men and the five puny horses across the river. Two men and their supplies would come across, and one man would go back. They had learned enough, or were weak enough, that no one got excited and capsized any of the canoes. M. Crooks's men are very weak, especially four of them, which is why we waited an extra day.

Three of the men decided to stay and live with the Shoshone and take up trapping later, when their strength returns. Our group is now made up of 35 men, two boys, my Pierre's kicking daughter, and me. And the five skinny horses. At least my horse has been able to eat while we camp.

We are finally all together on the same shore and ready to finish this journey. I no longer think my daughter will be born at Fort Astoria; I now only hope she is born on the Columbia River and not in these mountains. Though, mostly, I just want her born and healthy. As much as I do not like her kicking, I worry when she does not.

These mountains are barren, like the plains we just crossed. Trees are few and far apart, unless there is a creek or river. It is snowing.

No. 148 - *24 December 1811*

Again, the guides refused to lead us until Paul blessed them, and only then did they lead us from the river and up a trail over the hills. Sometimes the trail is smooth and easy, and sometimes it is even and level. It is a good trail, except for the snow.

The snow fell sometimes and sometimes it rained. Sometimes it did both together.

I let my Pierre lead the horse. I do not have the energy to even guide her. I am too tired, and too cold, to write more this night.

No. 149 - *28 December 1811*

Paul rides behind me. I welcome his warmth and support against my back. We crossed some mountains this morning and are now in a long, wide valley. A little river wanders through the valley. In the summer, it must be beautiful; now it is too cold and too white, all covered in snow. I am thankful the sun is not out, or we would all suffer from aching eyes and be unable to see where we go.

No. 150 - 30 December 1811

We are still in the beautiful valley and found six Shoshone tipis with plenty of horses. M. Hunt bought four horses, three dogs, and some roots they had dried.

They then showed our guides the pass we needed to take.

My bones are grinding. Paul sings over me with his rattle. I long for the warmth of a tipi. The women do not invite me.

No. 151 - 31 December 1811

My Pierre and the boys stayed with me. The baby came easily, and after he was born, my Pierre let me sleep a bit as I held the baby to my breast. Too soon, though, he woke me and lifted us onto the horse. I named him in my heart after Father Lark, Little Lark, and held him in my left arm, Paul rode in the sling at my side, and Jean-Jean rode behind. We had to catch up with M. Hunt and the men, or we would surely die alone in this cold, white, and forsaken place.

Before we left, Paul shook his rattle over us all. Little Lark is quiet and nurses but a little, then fusses, and then sleeps. I think I have little milk. My Pierre led the horse, and we caught up with the group on the edge of a forest.

They were surprised to see us, and the men were very curious about Little Lark. It was funny to see some of them tickle his cheek with their fingers and coo at him. The baby fussed and looked to me.

The fire they had going was very welcome. My Pierre lifted me off the horse and set me near the fire. One of the men put his pack behind me so I could lean back and rest. The baby was warm under my robes and slept.

No. 152 - 1 January 1812

The guides and M. Hunt were ready to leave this morning, but the French voyageurs wanted a day to celebrate the New Year. They said no self-respecting Frenchman would travel this day. A big fire was set, and there was much singing and dancing. I did not miss the travel and slept as much as I could.

Little Lark fusses softly, then is quiet, and then fusses more. I fear my milk is not as plentiful as it should be. It is good, I think, that he sleeps a lot and does not cry.

The guides say we will be down out of the mountains, and the snow, and in the village in just a few days. I hope Little Lark gets enough milk until then. Maybe I can find a woman who will nurse him for me once we are there.

My Pierre says he is not disappointed, that our next baby will be a girl. Besides, he says, a man can never have too many sons. Jean-Jean and Paul like to hold their little brother. Jean-Jean wants to teach him how to use a bow and arrow. Paul tries to teach him to sing.

No. 153 - 4 January 1812

We reached a point today where we were as high as all the

other mountains around us, and then we began going downhill. Part of the slopes around us are wooded, some are bare.

The cold is bitter, and the clouds are dark and heavy. I smell snow in the air. The men asked Paul to rattle us up some warmer weather. He smiled and began a dance and chant for them.

The guides say we will soon be not only out of the mountains, but also out of the snow.

No. 154 - 6 January 1812

The sun came out for the first time since we climbed into the mountains. The men are now sure Paul possesses strong medicine.

The snow has gone away, and far to the west we can see more plains. It is good to be out of the snow.

Little Lark is not well. He sleeps more and more. He tries to nurse, but he has little strength, and I have little milk.

My Pierre carries him some of the time, and the sadness in his face tells me what my heart knows. Paul shakes his rattle over the baby and sings to him. But his song is a death song, not a life song. I can tell because it is so mournful, even though he sings in a language I do not understand. I hope he lives until we reach the village of Sciatogas and Tushepaks. Maybe a woman with milk will nurse him.

No. 155 - 7 January 1812

Paul sang for the guides this morning, and then sang to his baby brother, who opened his eyes and smiled. My heart soared. My joy, my hope, was to be short-lived.

We came to a stream that led us through a very narrow pass through three mountains and were finally out of the snow. The banks were covered in horsetails and we found many herds of black-tail deer, though no one could get close enough to kill any.

While my Pierre and I stopped at the top of a hill overlooking a great plain, I realized our baby had died. He sleeps now with the Great Spirit. When I told Pierre, he held the baby, then gave him back to me, and walked a way off the trail where he dug a hole. When it was to his satisfaction, he lined it with pine needles, cut the front from his red wool shirt, and carefully wrapped the tiny, still form in it before placing him in the grave.

When the men realized what happened, and what we had done, they gathered rocks for the top of the grave and stood by us, giving what support they could. Pierre repeated a prayer from his childhood, "*Sainte Marie, Mère de Dieu, priez pour nous, pauvres pécheurs, maintenant et à l'heure de notre mort. Amen.*" While my Pierre recited the prayer, Paul took his feather and laid it on top of the grave, then put another rock on top.

Tears fall from my eyes, and I hug my boys close to me and am grateful they still live.

It is night and we are encamped near the grave. Paul asked me to take him back to the grave, where he sang a soft and mournful death song for his brother. Now both my tiny son and Father Lark are dead to me.

Several of the men have yet to arrive at camp. M. Hunt says we traveled 68 miles. My Pierre has set up our camp, and I long for the comfort of his arms wrapped about me.

I did not say it, but I wondered if Little Lark would have lived if M. Hunt had listened to his guides.

No. 156 - 8 January 1812

Paul sang again for our guides before they led us down a steep little creek to the floor below and the village of Sciatogas and Tushepaks.

The little creek met a larger river, the Umatilla, where the village is situated. We could see huge herds of horses off in the distance, maybe as many as 2,000.

These people have tipis made of mats and wear good clothing, buffalo robes or deerskin shirts and leggings, richly adorned with colorful beads and shells, and stones.

They are a tall and proud people, clean and honest. They are very good traders, although they can be generous, too. One of the families moved out of their tipi so my Pierre, the boys, and I could have a place alone. They went to be with her mother. That was the nicest of gifts. And my Pierre lets me rest. That, too, is a nice gift.

M. Hunt says we will stay a few days before continuing our journey, which will give stragglers a chance to catch up to us and to get some much needed rest. The Cayuse tell us we are only two days down the Umatilla to the Columbia.

Our guides are eager to return home to their families, but M. Hunt has asked them to stay until he can get good horses for them in payment for their services. They have agreed but ask him to please be quick, as they have women and children who wait for their return.

My little medicine man has barely gone from my side since his brother was born, and he looks at me with those huge owl eyes but says nothing. When I sleep, I hear him shake his rattle softly and sing a life song over me.

No. 157 - 10 January 1812

By ones and twos the men have been arriving off the mountain. By dark last night, all were here, exhausted, hungry, but safe.

Pierre and I have cried in private, holding each other. Although it is a part of life, this death is still so hard. I think my Pierre holds M. Hunt responsible. Had he listened to his guides, we would not have starved so much, and I would have had women to help. This is just one more thing to grumble about.

Yesterday, Pierre and M. Hunt went to see the Cayuse. I stayed, shivering under the robes. Paul sang me a song of life, and I slept. I woke to the smell of smoke from sweet grass and sage. A strange man sat next to me, wafting the smoke over me with a feather, chanting a song. A young girl and Paul were on either side of him.

The girl dipped a cloth in cool water and bathed my face, then handed me a bowl of something to drink. It was bitter, but I drank it all.

The man signed that Paul had found him and brought him to me. He signed that Paul has strong medicine, and that I will be fine.

When I opened my eyes later, the shivering had stopped, and Paul handed me another bowlful of bitterness to drink again. When I opened my eyes again, it was this morning, and I felt better. I could even smile.

No. 158 - 11 January 1812

Jean-Jean stayed to play with some new friends as Paul and I went to the tipi of the medicine man. He began to teach us his language, or as much as he could. By good fortune, many of the signs are the same or similar from tribe to tribe.

Of course, he could not teach us all his language but enough so we could communicate with the help of signing. I think he told us about their creation. I could not understand all of it, but the coyote and horse are holy to them. They believe dogs are descended from the coyote, so they, too, are sacred.

The women were kind, and though shrewd traders with the men, they were generous with the boys and me, giving us food, and leather for moccasins. One woman even gave me a dress. It belonged to her daughter who had outgrown it, but it fit me fine.

I am much shorter than the Cayuse and, right now, thinner than I have been in years.

My Pierre was not pleased about the dress; he is a proud man and thinks he should provide everything. I told him it was a loan, and when we come back this way, I would bring one in return. At that, he softened. My other dress was worn out. I cut what could be used to make the boys vests or moccasins.

It is good to be in a village, around people who are generous with their provisions. We slowly regain our strength. And our knowledge of these people grows by the day. The woman who gave me the dress showed me some of their designs with beads and quills

My Pierre and I have talked, and when M. Hunt goes back to Saint Louis, we think we may not return with him but stay somewhere in this Oregon Country. If our mothers still live, they have sons and daughters close to care for them. I would like to see Anna and Father Lark and tell them of our journey, but I do not want to repeat the journey to do so. My Pierre does not want to repeat the journey, either.

I would not mind ending our journey here with the Cayuse. My Pierre says we may come back, but we are so close, now, it would be foolish not to see this fabled Astoria. I agree with him. We have suffered too much not to see the proper end of our journey. Besides, he will not be paid the rest of his money until we reach Fort Astoria.

No. 159 - 12 January 1812

Paul and the medicine man have developed a strong bond. Paul has picked up the language quickly, and he and the medicine man spend many hours talking and chanting. The medicine man wants Paul to stay with him and his family, to be raised and properly trained. I am not comfortable with this arrangement, but my Pierre says it will be all right for a few days. But the Cayuse take slaves, and I fear I may not get Paul back. The man gave us his son to keep Jean-Jean company, and as a hostage for Paul. I feel awkward, but the boy enjoys playing with Jean-Jean, and teaching him the language.

The Cayuse language is very difficult, and even they seldom speak it any more, preferring the simpler Nez Perce language, which they have adopted, and that is what we learn. It will stand us in good stead in our travels, they say. Even so, it is difficult, and we learn only basic words and get by with them and by signing.

The Cayuse moved their village today about 15 miles farther down the Umatilla, and Paul went with them. I asked Paul before he left why they were moving, but he just shrugged his shoulders. They are not far, and we will stop for our son on our way to the mighty Columbia and the final part of our journey.

I think they moved because dog and horse are sacred to them, and they do not allow them to be killed or eaten in their villages. Now, we can kill and eat them both and not break their rules about forbidden food.

The kindness and generosity the Cayuse show us will not soon be forgotten. It will be with great sadness on my part when we must leave. However, the stay has given all of us a much-needed rest and the recuperation of our strength and stamina.

Jean-Jean is not happy that Paul has gone. I think he is jealous none of his new friends invited him to go and stay with them, but he is happy that now he has a brother his own age. At least until we again begin our journey, and retrieve Paul.

No. 160 - 15 January 1812

M. Hunt was able to purchase eight horses and two colts from the Cayuse. They were not the best of their herds, which was fine with us. They cost less. We ate the two colts. I think the Cayuse knew we would eat them, and rather than forbid it, they moved their village.

M. Hunt gave two of the horses to our guides in payment of their services. They rode to the village with us, to ask Paul to sing for them before going back over the mountains. The medicine man added his song, so they received a double blessing.

The medicine man was impressed the guides came to Paul and asked for his blessing, and Paul was both pleased and sad. He liked the guides, and now they were leaving instead of coming to Fort Astoria with us, as he had hoped.

Some of our men managed to buy horses, but they were very expensive, and not the best from the Cayuse herds. They could be ridden, however, and the men would not have to walk so far. Some of the men shared the cost of the horses and would share the riding.

The Cayuse also had venison for sale at the village, but they charged a great deal for it, and we did not buy any. Instead we bought fish and dogs, but did not eat either dog or horse in their village. We will save them for the trail.

No. 161 - 21 January 1812

The last two days were a slow and easy journey, as many of the men are still very weak, but we have at last reached the shores of the mighty Columbia. Never have I seen such a river! It is wide and fast and should get us to Fort Astoria quickly, once we get canoes. The Cayuse told M. Hunt not to get canoes until after we pass the Great Falls. They also told him to cross the Columbia at Wallula, where the Walla Walla River joins the Columbia, and to travel the north shore. I do not know why.

M. Hunt told the men we have traveled 1,751 miles since leaving Saint Louis and lived through unbelievable hardship and privations. He did not think to include that my Pierre and I had lost a child and the boys a brother.

The boys and I are seldom even seen by M. Hunt. He did not want us to come along, but we came, anyway. He may not see us, but we see him. And we hear him, and whether he speaks French or English, we now understand him. He has not learned the art of keeping his emotions from his face.

The people here have very little. They are neither clean nor proud like the Cayuse, but they are generous. They have little but gave us many of their salmon trout to eat. For their generosity, Paul sang for them. They were appreciative of Paul's songs and dance.

The salmon trout is a red-meated fish, oily, and very rich. Most of us prefer dog or horse, but once in a while, the salmon is good, especially when smoked. The jerky made from it is delicious to eat on the trail.

Paul and Jean-Jean often ride the horse my Pierre bought, I both walk and ride. I despair we will ever get canoes again. The voyageurs wonder if they will remember how to hold and use a paddle. Then they begin to sing the paddle song and move their arms as if we were canoeing down the trail.

No. 162 - 23 January 1812

We encamped near Wallula, a village of about 50 canoes. Before we crossed to the north bank, M. Hunt bought more fish and nine dogs that were fat and delicious. They were a welcome treat after so much of the salmon trout.

The trail is very good, easy to see and follow, and the weather is beautiful and mild. It feels good to be in dry air and sunshine after the last few months. The 12 miles we traveled seemed easy and fast.

The hills that come down to the river are barren of trees but covered in thick grasses. At the shore are cottonwoods and willows. The rivers provide the main source of food—fish. And there are many rivers and creeks that join the Columbia. For now, the trail is wide and gentle, but I long for canoes, as do the voyageurs.

My Pierre's mood has lifted some, too. But at night, we hold each other, sharing our sorrow with touch and tender words. My man may have a temper, but he loves his family very much.

The winds are strong today, and bring much dust and dirt. Sometimes the air is brown with it and our eyes hurt from so much grit being blown into them. We all cry to clear our eyes. Mud runs down our cheeks.

No. 163 - 28 January 1812

We followed the river all day, almost directly west. We had gone some distance when Paul stiffened and pointed in the direction we traveled. Soon we came upon a village. The people said they had deer and elk to sell but wanted too much in payment.

M. Hunt bought more dogs. Paul remained quiet and stiff the whole time we were there and kept going in a circle, pointing.

One of the men said that at the mouth of the river a white man built a house surrounded by stakes. He, himself, had not seen it but had heard of it from others who had been there. Does he mean Fort Astoria? I again hope we will soon be there. I know I am not alone in that hope.

Some of the men we met stole the ropes with which our horses were tethered. The horses escaped, and we spent a great deal of time getting them back.

We are back in the mountains again, mountains bare of trees, with many sheer drops, but beautiful.

In the last days, we came almost 60 miles. The winds have died down, and the air is again clear. Many of the people we see have sores on their eyes. It must be from the dust. I hope we do not get them.

It is hard to accept these people and their dishonesty after living among the Cayuse who are so close to them. I smile at the idea of a Sioux and Cayuse war party swooping out of the hills to teach these people proper manners.

No. 164 - 29 January 1812

The mountains are close and the rocks are more numerous, though the trail is still good. It is wide and well-traveled, easy for both the men and the horses.

Paul pointed many times, and each time we could see men on horses. When we camped tonight, we set up a night watch. The tribes we have met along the river think stealing is an honorable way of life. It makes us wary and on edge. We are not used to such people. At home, dishonesty is dealt with harshly; here it seems to be a matter of pride.

Paul danced a circle around the horses after they were tethered and shook his rattle. It was funny to watch, but no one laughed. They thanked him.

Because of the mountains, we only walked 15 miles today. Although we are in a hurry, M. Hunt realizes the men are still recovering and does not push us. The men look at the river with longing. We all want canoes to ride in again.

No. 165 - 30 January 1812

Many, many people—the Tou-et-ka—came across the Columbia to visit and dance in our honor. They live at the mouth of the Deschutes. There were so many, our men became suspicious and nervous. When M. Hunt claimed he was sick, they soon departed and took their canoes back across the river.

Paul did not seem to mind them as much as the men we met earlier, but we have all become suspicious of these river tribes, and we are not willing to trust any of them.

My Pierre has taken to standing guard over our campsite when any of them get too close. Jean-Jean stands next to him, his bow in his hands and his quiver on his back.

As lonely as I am for a woman to talk with, I am not interested in these women. It may be a mistake on my part, but after the thievery of the earlier tribes, I am very cautious. I mentioned my idea to Pierre about the war parties teaching them manners, and Jean-Jean overheard me and said he would do that. That we do not need the Sioux or the Cayuse. His father laughed, and grabbed him in a big hug.

No. 166 - 31 January 1812

When we passed the Great Falls, there was so much water going over we could not see the other side because of the mist. Once past the falls, we could look back and see the whole of them. They are magnificent. The locals call them the Celilo Falls. They say when the fish go up and over the falls, the men stand on rocks and platforms and catch the fish with nets—truly a sight to behold.

It did not take much time before we reached Wishram, the name of the village at the east entrance to a long and narrow gorge. Although the river goes through the gorge fast, it is nothing—at least what we can see—like the narrow gorges on the Snake River.

The people we met seem very smart, and some speak English, at least a little. They told us that M. Stuart, one of the men who went out on his own when the party separated, had been here and gone up a northern tributary to set up a winter camp. It is good to know he made it and is alive.

There is a tall, pointy mountain, covered in snow that M. Hunt tells us is called Mount Hood. It looks almost close enough to reach out and touch.

The river is very turbulent after the falls, but we have been told by the locals it is navigable by canoe from here all the way to Fort Astoria and the Big Water.

No. 167 - 1 February 1812

Paul stiffened, pointed, and turned around and around, and soon we found ourselves surrounded by many men. It was hard to tell how many, as they kept moving, but I think there must have been more than 30. They carried knives and axes, and we felt quite threatened by their menacing gestures. They spoke, but none of us knew what they said, and they made no attempt to help us understand. We quickly set up armed guards. Once the guards were in place, the men left.

Paul relaxed a little. But it was obvious he did not want us here. I agree with him.

If these people steal our goods, will they try to steal us? Especially the boys? I have talked with my Pierre, and he agrees, we will not let the boys wander off or go to the villages to seek friends but will keep them with us, or at least with our men.

No. 168 - 2 February 1812

While M. Hunt talked with the tribesmen and the rest of our men stood guard, and even though Paul pointed, some of the tribesmen still managed to steal an axe, and they followed us, looking for an opportunity to steal even more. Even with the guards, they were able to steal two guns and a horse in the middle of the night.

Paul felt bad his medicine had not protected us, but the men and I assured him it was not his fault, he could only do so much, and that his medicine saved everything else.

Most importantly, no one was stolen or injured. What kind of people are these who steal and take pride in it? Why have the Cayuse not come down and cleaned these people out? Should we visit again, I may ask them. It would be doing everyone a favor, I think.

No. 169 - 3 February 1812

M. Hunt traded horses and supplies for a canoe and went downriver with some of the men. He said he would meet us at the mouth of the Klickitat River. We have now joined him near the Klickitat village there. He had purchased three canoes to take us the rest of the way to Fort Astoria. He asked Pierre to camp with the group, as these men were thieves, but Pierre thought he would be safe because I am an Indian and they would not steal from another Indian.

He will not listen to anyone, my stubborn husband. And I know better than to argue with him. If M. Reed, or anyone else had made the suggestion, I think he would have seen the wisdom in it, but he sees no wisdom in anything said by M. Hunt. I say nothing. With luck, the horse will still be there in the morning when we get up.

While M. Hunt traded, the river men stole a tomahawk and our last axe. I will not miss these people, and hope the people near Fort Astoria are more honorable than these.

Paul points to them and says, "Bad." He makes sure his tomahawk and gourd are still on my belt.

No. 170 - 4 February 1812

My Pierre tethered my horse outside our tent, but it was stolen in the middle of the night. Now we cannot even trade it. I say nothing. Paul just looks at him with his round and accusing eyes. Best to stay out of Pierre's way when something like this happens. His anger is not to be trifled with.

M. Hunt says the winds are again too violent for us to continue today, so we will stay over until they die down. He traded a horse for another canoe.

We will not let the boys go into the village to play. The boys do not even ask to go into the village. Jean-Jean pays attention when Paul points at it, and at the people as they come near, and says, "Bad!" So do I. So do the men.

No. 171 - 5 February 1812

It started raining and has gotten worse, and the nearby hills, at least what we can see of them, are covered in snow. The rain is not like the rain on the prairie. There it comes and goes. Here it just comes and stays. Not a hard rain but a constant rain, and everything is wet. It is impossible to keep anything dry.

We came to another village and traded the last three horses for two more canoes. We will make the rest of the trip on the river.

The boys are excited, and the voyageurs are happy, even though the winds keep us here. My Pierre carved each boy a paddle, and they sit on a log paddling their make-believe canoe while singing Alouette. Sometimes one or two of the voyageurs join them and tell them to watch out for that rock, to beware of those rapids. It is a great game for all.

The boys do not get in the way of the men, and do not pester them, so they are not only accepted, but their company is often welcome and ofttimes requested.

No. 172 - *10 February 1812*

The winds finally died down, and as soon as M. Hunt told us we would leave, Paul went to the river and sang and shook his rattle at each canoe. As soon as he determined which one I would ride in, he crawled in and sat down. At last, we are underway!

We went about 15 miles until we reached a large rapids. M. Hunt decided not to chance losing anything more, so we landed and by late morning, we were portaged below the rapids.

The boys were disappointed; they wanted to go through the white water like they had practiced on their log. They were promised they would get the opportunity later, as there surely would be more of the white water up ahead.

The trees along the shore have again changed; there are oak and ash. The air is wetter, and the hills are covered in dark green and pointy trees. In this constant mist, they appear almost black.

Looking up at the hills, it is interesting to watch the mist and clouds float above and through the mountains. They look so soft, like nothing I have seen before.

No. 173 -11 February 1812

This time, we had to portage about eight miles. I carried Paul; Jean-Jean walked. He carried some of my load, not much, but whatever he carried was one more thing I did not have to carry.

The hills are smaller and do not seem to have snow on them, or at least not much and the river is wider.

I am tired of having this constant mist in my face. No matter which way I turn, it is in my face. It is cold and wet, but better than the snow and rain of the mountains, so I will not complain. Besides I doubt anyone enjoys it. At least we have water and do not thirst. Nor do we hunger.

We stopped for the night, and Paul shook his rattle at the sky. I think he wanted the clouds and the rain and the fog to go away. He was ignored.

No. 174 - 13 February 1812

The mist has changed to rain, hail, and snow. I do not think

Grandfather Sky liked Paul's song very much.

We passed two rivers today, first the Sandy River, then the Willamette, where we espied many things cavorting in the Columbia. At first we thought they were people swimming in the cold water, but M. Reed, who is in our canoe, said they are seals that come up from the ocean. The boys are delighted to watch them swim, and Jean-Jean wants to swim, too.

M. Reed pointed out river otters. They are smaller and swim closer to the shore, but both seem mildly curious about us. We have, of course, seen otters but not the seals. They look like curious children as they play in the river.

By the time we crossed the mouth of the Willamette River, the Columbia was more than a mile wide. The shores are vast and covered in reeds, with small meadows and ponds to be seen on them as well as many forests, some with trees that lose their leaves, some with trees that never lose them.

The seals are more numerous, and curious. The boys want to pet them, but they do not come close enough. I would have to tell them no. This way, they can still enjoy watching the seals cavort without my having to say no.

Jean-Jean put his hand in the water and decided it is too cold for him to swim with the seals, so he is content, for now, to just watch them play around us.

We traveled about 52 miles today.

No. 175 - *14 February 1812*

We are very close now to Fort Astoria and the end of our

journey. It is hard to write because the ceaseless mist and fog makes everything, including the paper, damp. M. Reed says the constant moisture is why everything here grows such a dark green, and why there is so much game to be seen. He assures us we will not go hungry in this land of plenty!

We are again in mountains, but not as high as before.

No. 176 - *15 February 1812*

We stopped at a village today and met four men from Fort Astoria. They told us we would be there tomorrow and to camp on one of the low islands near the south bank of the river. We passed several large islands today. The north bank of the river is covered in oak and ash trees, but all had their roots in the river.

Fort Astoria! We will be there tomorrow. Everyone is so excited, but I am quiet. I cannot help but wonder how different it would have been if we had not had so many delays, if Little Lark might have lived, if, if.... Too many ifs. Little Lark is dead, and there is nothing my Pierre or I can do about it. Even in the best of circumstances, he might not have lived. Babies just die, sometimes.

M. Hunt said we went about 27 miles today.

No. 177 - *16 February 1812*

It rained all night, and a thick fog is upon us. As no one slept well and we are all eager to be on the river, as soon as it was light we were seated in the canoes. The fog was so thick we could hardly breathe, let alone see any distance, and it soaks through our clothes. But we are almost at our journey's end, so though the fog dampens our bodies, it cannot touch our spirits.

The boys and I decided to find something about this damp fog to like. We agreed it lets us be in our own little world. We made up stories about what is just beyond our sight. Cities that fade in the sunshine, deer willing to die that we might eat, strawberry bushes that always produce ripe berries. The boys enjoy the stories they make up and tell each other.

In the afternoon, the fog lifted, and we discovered it was high tide, and we paddled against the current. As soon as the tide began to drop, the current of the river began to push us toward our goal, instead of holding us back.

M. Hunt had explained tides a couple of days earlier when he realized we were in tidal waters. I had never heard of such a thing. We do not have tides on the Muddy; it just flows to the Mississippi.

We were in a large bay, with Fort Astoria on its south bank. Paul detected it first and pointed. All we could see was the stockade around the fort. It seemed to rest barely above the high-tide mark.

M. Reed said Fort Astoria is very close to the old Fort Clatsop, which Lewis and Clark built. He said we would have used that fort, but it was already falling apart, as nothing lasts long here, because of the constant damp. He said the old fort is about five miles away, up the Netul River, and we can go sometime later.

We were seen, and the men inside Fort Astoria came out to greet us, help pull the canoes ashore, and unload the supplies. I can hardly believe we are here!

Our journey ends with us in a large room, with a few smaller rooms off one end. It is heaven. It reminds me of home and Holy Rainbow. Even the noise of the men as they slap each other on the back, and laugh, and call, is welcome. We are here! We will sleep under a roof, out of the weather, for the first time in many months, and with a welcome fire for warmth.

As happy as the men were that we had made it here, we were that happy to discover that Messrs. McKenzie and McClellan have been here almost a month. They both expressed condolences when they realized our baby had died. Most of the men offered sympathy on the trip, when it happened, all but M. Hunt.

I admit, I took a certain delight when M. Hunt discovered his journal was a day off, that it was really the 15th of February, not the 16th. It is not a big thing, but one finds pleasure where one can. I think even Father Lark would smile.

When M. Reed asked M. Hunt how far we had come, I think all of us were surprised at his answer. He said that from Saint Louis to here we had traveled 3,500 very hard and rough miles.

Many of us were not allowed to stay in the fort and were taken a mile or two away to a settlement at Young's Bay to live with other Indians, Métis, and some people called Hawaiian from far across the Big Water. They seem friendly, but keep mostly to themselves.

No. 179 - 15 March 1812

We have been here for a month. The fort, and the settlement at Young's Bay, are filled with fleas! Everyone suffers from them. M. Reed said it never gets cold enough here to kill them off, and they live in the floors and the ground under the tipis and lodges and come out at night when we sleep.

I put cedar on all the floors. I do not know if it helps, but at least I am doing something, and the men say it is working. I change the cedar once a week. I would like to package the fleas and send them to the thieving river people. When I told M. Reed that, he laughed and asked if I had not noticed that is where the fleas began, about the time of the Great Falls. As I thought about it, I realized he was right. They deserve the fleas — we do not.

The ocean is huge. M. Reed took a group of us, including the boys, to see it. He called the big waves breakers. They are powerful, beautiful, and noisy. He says when a storm blows in they can reach very high, and showed us where trees had been tossed by those giant waves. Although we are not far from the ocean, we cannot hear it. When the storms blow in, the tops of the waves on the river turn white and stand higher, and that is enough for me. I am glad we came overland, and not by ship.

We do not get our water from the Columbia, because it is tidal and the water is brackish, but there are many small streams and rivers in the area, so good, sweet, drinking water is plentiful. And the rain, which we catch in barrels the men have built and set out.

Some of the men have gone to the beach to make salt.

They must travel about a day, and when they get there, they boil kettles of salt water until the water is gone, leaving the salt, which is then scraped out and packaged for cooking or preserving.

The sun, weak and watery, has shone a few days; the air is filled with moisture, even when there is no fog or rain. And everything is green, all year. Against the dark evergreen trees, the oak and other trees are a pale green as they begin to leaf out. And damp. Everything is damp, even in the fort.

The boys are happy to be free to walk and run and play. Paul no longer allows anyone to carry him unless he is too tired to walk.

We have our own place, and Paul's rattle and tomahawk are by his blanket. The medicine man of the Cayuse gave him a medicine bag. As he wears it under his shirt, I did not see it until I made him a new shirt. When I did see it and asked about it, he just smiled. His head and face are still that of an old man, but he is a happy child and getting stronger.

Food is not as scarce, and Pierre and a couple of the men have brought in many deer and elk. Every so often one or two of the men from M. Crooks's group straggle in, worn, weary, and starving. We are always joyful to see them and quickly give them food and new clothes.

I am settling into a routine and am kept busy with the hides. Most I prepare for shipment back east; but from some, I make moccasins and vests for the men. I also cook for them. In truth, I am running the household side of the fort where I am not allowed to live.

No. 180 - 11 May 1813

The last two from our group, Messrs. Ramsey Crooks and John Day, straggled into the fort today. Actually, they were brought in by some men of the fort who found them on the Columbia a few days earlier. They were ragged and hungry, and we welcomed them with great cheer and a hot meal.

My Pierre has been hired to hunt and act as interpreter, and I have been hired to act as the factotum of the fort and interpret when necessary. The boys and I quickly learned the trade language, *chinuk wawa*, or Chinook Jargon as it is called by the Europeans.

The boys run and play, though I notice Paul does not go far into the forest. My Pierre has told both boys not to, as the trees and undergrowth are very dense. It would be easy for them to get lost and not find their way back. Jean-Jean, I think, goes in and hides from his brother.

No. 181 - 1 June 1812

Paul has decided it is more fun to run than to walk and is picking up the local languages, including English, quickly. Faster even than Jean-Jean. Jean-Jean will ask a question or make a statement in one language. Paul gets them all mixed up, starting in French, then switching to *chinuk wawa* and ending in English.

The local people all speak different languages and have developed *chinuk wawa* as a means to communicate and trade with each other and the Europeans who come into the area. *Chinuk wawa* is easy to learn, far easier than the

English some of the men teach me.

Pierre says we will be here for at least another year. That is a great comfort to me, although I will be very busy, and he will often be gone for days at a time. This place grows on us, and we have decided we do not wish to return home. The boys are healthy, and Paul is growing into his face. Anna, I think, would be happy. I know I am.

No. 182 - 1 January 1813

It is a party time, and all the men are gathered to dance and sing and eat. I have been cooking for days to get ready, and the boys are very excited.

I have made everyone a pair of moccasins. Earlier, one of the men killed and skinned a porcupine and gave it to me. I pulled the quills and found enough roots, bark, and berries to dye them, so there is a little bead work on each pair. The boys each have new leggings and shirts to go along with their moccasins. Pierre gave me a bear hide last fall and told me to make something warm from it. I have made vests for the boys and myself.

The men have found a way to make fermented juice. There is only enough for each to have a small amount, so my Pierre will not become drunk or mean. When it was poured into the cups, they all turned to me and said, "To Madame Dorion. Thank you for taking such good care of us!" Then they cheered three times. My Pierre beamed.

The men allowed Jean-Jean and Paul to join in the dancing, though Paul mostly just ran around. Jean-Jean did a fair job. He has been practicing, I think.

Much has happened these past months. There is some kind of competition between the Astorians and the Canadians, but I do not understand it and do not really care. Everyone is healthy, and that is all that matters to me.

It is late, and the boys and I are tired and ready for bed. We shall go to our home and leave the men to celebrate without us.

Part III

Trapping on the Boise River

1813–1814

No. 183 - *5 May 1813*

M. Reed is talking with some of the men about returning to the Boise River to trap. My Pierre wants to go. I admit I would not mind going though it will be cold in the winter. At least it will be drier than here. I do not think this part of the country ever gets totally dry, even on sunny days, of which there are few. The men tell me it is sunnier farther inland, but I do not know. It is so foggy here.

The rain is not like the rain back home. This rain is softer, fills the air, and stays day after day. Clothes are never totally dry, once taken away from the fire. The moisture collects on the wool and leather, then beads and runs down. No one seems to mind, but the damp is monotonous. Everything smells old, and stale.

No. 184 - *12 June 1813*

M. Reed has hired both my Pierre and me to return to the Boise River with him to trap beaver. Jean-Jean is not happy to leave his friends, but Paul is excited. He wants to see his friend, the medicine man, and learn new medicine. I have much to do before we leave.

In the group will be Pierre Delaunay, Giles LeClerc, Andre La Chappelle, Jean Baptiste Turcotte, and Francois

Landry – all voyageurs. All but Delaunay are men of good spirit who love to laugh. My Pierre and two other men will be the hunters on the trip. Once we arrive, everyone will hunt and trap.

The boys will just be boys, though they will help as they are able. Jean-Jean wants to learn to trap, and I think my Pierre will take him some of the time. He is old enough to learn but not yet strong enough to set the traps by himself.

I will cook and act as interpreter and run the main post as I do here, except the boys and I will be allowed to live in the fort, once it is built, not forced to live outside it.

No. 185 - 15 June 1813

We will take only enough meat with us so that we will all ride in the canoes until we get to the Cayuse village to buy horses to go over the mountains.

It was cool and foggy when we set out this morning, but once away from the ocean, the fog lifted and the sun came out. There really is a sun here!

I can see where this trip will have challenges that the first one did not—Paul is no longer content to sit in the canoe. He wants to run everywhere and begs to be allowed to run along the river's edge.

I love the green of this side of the Cascade Mountains, but I will not miss the constant rain and drizzle. It seems to never end, though it does now and then—the changes often startle in their suddenness and beauty. But I look forward to the dry and open country once we reach the Great Falls and travel beyond them.

No. 186 - 24 June 1813

Oh, the sight! We did not see this when we passed by in the winter on the north side. I was told the salmon trout were not running then, but they are now. I do not understand why they say the fish are running, when they have no feet, but that is what they say about the fish when they come from the ocean to lay their eggs where they themselves were once hatched.

The men have planks of wood wedged between rocks, with plank-and-netting walks out in the falls. They stand on these narrow platforms, and when the mighty salmon trout jump to go up and over the Falls, they reach out with nets and catch them! It is amazing they do not lose their balance and fall to their deaths.

In this manner, the men catch thousands of pounds of the fish, which they put in baskets and toss them from man to man until the baskets are on the shore. The women empty the baskets and toss them back to the men. The women then clean and filet the fish and place them on racks to smoke and dry for winter.

The boys, of course, want to go out and help and are quite upset they are not allowed to do so.

Now that we are through the mountains, it is very warm. The boys have stripped to breechclouts and moccasins. Paul wants only his moccasins, but I have convinced him he must wear at least the breechclout. I again wear a dress without sleeves.

The boys want to stay and become fishermen. They are not happy when we insist they come with us to our journey's end. Paul says if he cannot stay here, he will stay with the medicine man of the Cayuse.

After the portage around the falls, when we were back in the canoe singing and paddling, Jean-Jean decided he wants to be a voyageur, not a fisherman, after all.

No. 187 - *28 June 1813*

We arrived today at the Cayuse village, and Paul immediately went looking for his friend the medicine man. I am not surprised they remember each other. Paul still has his medicine bag. He carries his gourd now, but still insists I wear his tomahawk at all times in my belt.

The medicine man was delighted to see Paul, and this time, they conversed in *chinuk wawa*, a language they both know.

We will spend a few days and sell our canoes. This will allow each of our men to buy packhorses. Two also bought horses to ride. My Pierre says he will buy an extra packhorse for our supplies, which had been in one of the canoes, and another horse for the boys and me to share.

M. Reed talked about going up the Snake and taking a long and arduous route to the Boise River, but my Pierre and the men convinced him the quicker and easier way was to go over the mountains, retracing the way we came. The Cayuse told him the trail was wide enough for packhorses as well as travois should we desire to use them.

It took much talking on the part of my Pierre and the others, but M. Reed finally decided it made no sense to go the long way, when we would have few if any trails to follow. He admitted it was only because he wanted to check out the beaver. That someone joked and called him M. Hunt probably helped him decide to stick to his original plan.

We will take our time to sell our canoes and buy horses and whatever else we need to take back across the Blue Mountains.

I wonder if we will see Little Lark's grave. Perhaps by now it is known only to the Great Spirit.

No. 188 - 1 July 1813

Paul's friend was a big help to us. He helped not only in bargaining for the horses but also in acquiring a guide to show us a different and somewhat easier trail than going up the creek. The guide will only take us to the top of the hill and show us the trail.

We have our horses and supplies and are now camped at the base of the hill. Tomorrow, our guide will take us on the trail. It is a very steep hill, but they have carved out a trail wide enough for travois to safely make it, using switchbacks. It will be much better than when we came down the steep and narrow canyon last year. I am not sure we could have taken horses up that canyon.

The Cayuse medicine man joined our camp, once we assured him we would not kill or eat either dog or horse while he was there. He said he and Paul will sing for us before we leave in the morning.

The boys are now excited about the journey. Jean-Jean has again decided trapping will be more fun than fishing, and Paul just wants to meet new medicine men. He hopes to meet some of the Snake medicine men.

I told about the river people who practiced thievery as something to be prideful of and suggested maybe the Cayuse should consider teaching them a lesson in manners. He laughed and said they did not want the river fleas on their horses. He asked if we did not have a problem with fleas there, especially just past the Great Falls. I had to admit we did, but even there the fleas were not as bad as when we reached Fort Astoria.

No. 189 - *2 July 1813*

Tomorrow, we will pass Little Lark's resting place. My Pierre said if he could find it, he would stop and say a prayer. It will make my husband feel better to do this, but I know Little Lark is with the Great Spirit, and I have no need to see where he is buried or to say the prayer. I will go with my Pierre because I am his wife. And I am the mother of Little Lark. I still grieve my loss.

I can see it in his eyes—he, too, thinks of the baby we buried here. The little boy who will never run and play with his brothers. We are both quiet, wrapped in thoughts of our Little Lark.

The white men bury their dead and mark the place

with something and go back when they can. Often they talk to the dead as if they were still present and somehow could hear them and even possibly respond. It brings them a form of comfort.

When a person dies in my tribe, we no longer speak of him. His things are given away or burned. But Little Lark had no things, only the place in my heart where I carried him—where I carry him still, and though I may not speak of him, I will remember him always.

Even when my mother showed us where my father was, we did not speak of him, but I am sure she still remembers, if she still lives. I think of them both, often.

No. 190 - 5 July 1813

Paul found Little Lark's grave first. The feather he left for his brother was still anchored, though it was quite weather-worn, and several more rocks had been placed on top of it, along with things other people left on the grave: bits of cloth, three blue beads.

When the men realized why my Pierre and I stood by the mound of rocks, they joined us. Pierre repeated the prayer he said when we buried our infant son and then each man added a rock, and a gift. A bead, a piece of tobacco, something to help the spirit of the baby on his journey. Paul sang a song of joy and happiness, and as we left, he took my hand and said the baby was fine, not to worry.

I was not worried, only sad. It is hard to carry a baby for so long, only to lose it so soon after birth.

No. 191 - 1 August 1813

The trail is wide and easy, and well-marked. Our guides have returned to their homes, and we travel forward on our own. It is much prettier in the summer than in the winter when all was white with deep snow and bitter cold.

The boys and I have gathered berries and roots to add to our meals. We have met some friendly Shoshone and Nez Perce. They are quite impressed that we travel with our own medicine man, even if he is only four years old.

Game is plentiful, so we are well fed. The horses forage near the trail and remain fat and sleek. Compared to our last journey through these mountains, this one is easy and enjoyable.

No. 192 - 15 August 1813

We are once again on the banks of the Snake close to where the Boise River enters the larger river. The men are building a cabin as rapidly as they can on the bank of the Snake, near the mouth of the Boise River. This cabin will be used to store supplies and trade goods, as well as to shelter us during the winter months. The boys and I will stay here while the men are out at their camps setting their traps and hunting.

The boys help by clearing away brush the men do not need, bringing them their tools when asked, and water.

It is too late to plant the Three Sisters, but I will plant them next spring with the seeds I brought. I hope they will grow in this dirt.

My Pierre hunts and I cook. We have met a few friendly Snakes. They do not speak *chinuk wawa*, but I remember some of their language, and we sign.

No. 193 - 28 August 1813

Three of our trappers have died. The first, M. Turcotte died painfully of scrofula. No sooner had we buried him than M. Landry was thrown by his horse. His injuries were too severe for us to heal, and he died. Paul sang a death song for both men. These men were good trappers, of sunny disposition, and shall be missed.

Then M. Delaunay, a sullen and bitter man not given much to smiling or helping—never once did I see him laugh—deserted us in a fit of temper. No one knows what caused his anger; he just became angry and left. My Pierre told me a few days later he had seen M. Delaunay's scalp in the hands of an Indian. He recognized it by the color of hair and the ornament still in it.

I keep the boys close.

No. 194 - 5 September 1813

Before we vacated Fort Astoria, we were asked to watch for Messrs. John Hoback, Jacob Rezner, and Edward Robinson, who were believed to be in the Snake River area. They stumbled into our post yesterday, naked and more dead than alive. Jean-Jean was the first to see them, and when he recognized them, he let out a yell. They said hostiles had stripped them of all their worldly goods, everything they had. They counted it their good luck to have escaped with their lives. Jean-Jean looked very serious as he told them that if he had been there, they could have fought the Indians and won.

My Pierre had just returned from a hunt, and I had much food to serve the men. While they rested for a few days, I made them each new moccasins, leggings, and a winter shirt. They made their own robes from the hides.

When we arrived three weeks ago and built the first cabin, the locals were friendly, but soon after, when M. Reed refused to give them guns and ammunition, they became angry and hostile. M. Reed refused because they had committed two acts of hostility—they stole M. LaChapelle's long hooded capote and shot an arrow into the flank of one of our horses.

M. Reed and the men thought it prudent that we move to a new location and build another wintering house. I am glad I did not plant my garden.

No. 195 - 25 September 1813

We are now set up in a new place, about 15 miles up the Boise River. The new fort is almost complete, and the boys and I will stay here over the winter. I will cook when the men are in camp and dress the pelts they bring, as well as render the grease into tallow.

My Pierre says they will try not to be gone longer than five days at a time, ten at the most. M. Reed has tacked the calendar he made to the wall, so I can mark off the days as they pass. The men will build a small cabin upstream, closer to where the beaver have built their dams.

The men are gone scouting and reconnoitering the best places to set their traps. I am busy making everyone heavy clothes for the winter. Already the nights are cold, and the air has a chill during the day.

I am very busy with the cooking and sewing and getting the cabin livable and workable. The boys are a big help and do what they are asked the first time they are asked. I remember some of the American children in Saint Louis, who when asked to do something would whine and make excuses. I am so glad my boys do not do that. But then, I think my Pierre would raise his hand to them if they did.

It is too late to plant, but next spring, I shall plant the Three Sisters.

No. 196 - 1 January 1814

It is very late, but it is New Year, and I must write that we are all healthy and strong, and the men are bringing in prime pelts. Tonight, the boys danced and sang with the men until they dropped to the floor, exhausted. My Pierre put them in their bed. The cabin is now quiet, except for the snores of the men, and I am happy and about to be in the arms of my husband. It is so nice to have a warm cabin to live in during the winter.

No. 197 - 9 January 1814

The snow is falling, and it is hard to see very far. It is so very quiet. The snow muffles any noises that might be out there. The fire wood has been brought inside, and the new pelts are nearly dressed. They will be packed by the time the men return in two or three days and I will be ready to begin work on the new batch of pelts.

All day, Paul has paced and stopped and listened, then started all over again. He does not want to go out but says nothing is wrong. He does not want me to go out. I am jittery. M. Reed, who is still here and will leave in a couple of days with the other men, says it is just the unnatural quiet. He says it gets on everyone's nerves and not to worry.

The boys sleep, and the quiet is restful, if unnerving. We will have many pelts to sell this spring. My Pierre says he does not want to go back to the Missouri, which the French call the Muddy, that he is happy here and wants us to raise our family here. The land is harsh but bountiful. I like the country around the Umatilla better, but here is fine, too. As long as my Pierre is with me, I can live anyplace and be happy.

No. 198 - Cold Moon, 1814

Much has happened, little of it good. I will try to write of it, but the pain is almost too much to bear.

The day after my last entry, on 10 January 1814, a friendly Snake came to our cabin and told me some Snakes, called Dog-Rib Snakes, had burned the first cabin we built and were on their way to where my Pierre and the men are. He said they danced and sang war songs.

The boys and I quickly dressed in our warmest clothes, gathered what food we could carry, and set out to warn Pierre and the men, leaving M. Reed and the others. It soon became dark, and we got lost in the fading light and poorly marked trails.

The next day I discerned heavy smoke and thought it might be a village, so I hid the boys and myself in the bushes until that night. We decamped at first light the next morning and by late evening, came to the cabin the men had built. I hid the boys and studied the house. It was dark and quiet, and then I espied a man stagger a way off from the cabin. He acted like he was very sick and could barely walk.

I recognized him as M. LeClerc and went to him. He was badly wounded and had lost a great deal of blood, but he said that Messrs. La Chapelle and Rezner and my Pierre had been robbed and murdered that morning. The horses had been stolen or killed.

He told me not to go in, but I could see my Pierre on the floor, bloody and hacked. His scalp was gone. I wanted to run to him, to see if he still lived, to hold him, but M. LeClerc persuaded me not to, as there might still be Dog-Ribs in the cabin. There were.

I can write no more. The pain is too great. How could I leave my Pierre alone on the dirt of the cabin floor?

My heart is broken beyond repair.

No. 199 - *Cold Moon, 1814*

I have mourned as I can. It has been days since my last entry. Today I will try to write more. Maybe it will help if I can put the hurt of my heart onto the paper of my journal. Father Lark used to say that a hurt shared was a hurt halved. I will write and hope it halves my hurt.

LeClerc was right; there were Dog-Ribs in the cabin. While they ransacked the cabin, I hid LeClerc with the boys and crept back to the cabin. The ones who had stolen our horses had ridden on, but there were four horses tethered in the lean-to behind the cabin. It did not take much to catch two and send the others on their way. I walked the two I stole back to where LeClerc and the boys were hidden and managed to lift LeClerc onto one and the boys onto the other. Then I led them into the woods, where we would not be easily seen.

The next day, I could see people traveling eastward but

did not know if they were friendly, so we dismounted and stayed hidden until the travelers were out of sight. I managed to get LeClerc back on his horse, but he was weak, and after we traveled a ways, he fell off and his wounds opened again.

He was too weak to travel, so we stayed with him. Paul told him he would sing his death song when it was safe to do so. LeClerc smiled and died. We could not give him a proper burial but covered him with brush and snow and packed it as much as possible.

We arrived back at our home to find that M. Reed and the other men were all dead—scalped and tortured. Their bodies had been mutilated with axes, or maybe knives and spears.

I got the boys back into the woods and we hid through the night and the next day. Our food was now completely gone. We were hungry and cold, and because it was quiet and I saw no one else, I built a small fire for warmth, but put it out when the darkness came so no one would see the flames.

Will I ever forget seeing my Pierre, dead on the floor? My heart hurts, but writing out the hurt helps to lessen it. Or make it more bearable. Father Lark was right.

No. 200 - Hunger Moon, 1814

The boys stayed where I hid them, and I went back to the cabin and searched for food, gathering all the fish I could find and carry. I took a bearskin and some deer hides. As long as it was daylight, I thought a small fire would be safe and unseen. I took that chance and built a small fire long enough to cook some of the fish. Once dark began to settle, I put the fire out so it could not be seen, and we would not be found. I wondered if they knew we escaped and hunted us.

We stayed the next day, and the next night I went back for more fish and whatever meat I could find and carry.

My exertions and my sorrow were too much—I collapsed for what the boys later said was three days.

How could they have killed my Pierre? What will the boys and I do? How will we live?

Not knowing who to trust, the boys and I hid as much as possible. Jean-Jean and Paul each rode atop a packed horse, and I led the way. We made it back to the Snake River, forded it, then began the long trek back into the mountains.

There was no food for the horses, other than what they could find and eat, and when the first died, I butchered it, and we ate what we could of the meat and sucked the marrow from the bones. I packed the rest, what little there was of it, leaving the entrails for the wolves..

Jean-Jean remembered the friendly Shoshone from our earlier trip, and wondered if we could stay with them, but I am afraid. I am a lone woman now, with two children and no man to protect me. No, it would be too easy for them to kill my sons and make me a slave. We will stay hidden and survive, or die together.

No. 201 - Hunger Moon, 1814

I think we have crossed the summit, but the snow is still deep, unlike two years ago. I took us off the trail into the forest, and we have made our encampment. At first, I thought the snow seemed deeper than before because there are no men to break our trail. Now I am sure it is just deeper. I only know we can go no farther. The second horse has died.

I built our small wikiup of branches and hides, then covered it with snow. It would have been easier had I not lost Paul's tomahawk along the way, probably when we forded the river and I fell from the horse. We have to crawl into the wikiup, but with the cedar boughs on the ground we are above the cold and wet, and with the hide-covered branches above us, and snow on top of them, we have a little heat from our bodies and the small fires I light at the opening.

Baptiste, as Jean-Jean now wants to be called, and I set small traps to catch rabbits and squirrels so, though we are hungry, we are not starving. At least not yet.

Paul has sung the death songs of each of the men. His voice broke when he sang for his father. I asked if he would sing ours, and he said, no, we are not dead.

We are hungry. And cold. I just want to wake from this bad dream that never seems to end.

I want my Pierre.

PART IV

EPILOGUE

Epilogue

Marie and the boys survived. By March the weather had warmed enough that they were able to come down out of the Blue Mountains, possibly along today's Meacham Creek—a steep, narrow, north-running canyon.

The only implement Marie had was her knife, and it was dull. Their food was almost gone; they had eaten their horses and whatever frozen berries they could find. At one point she became snow blind for two or three days and could go nowhere. Jean Baptiste tried to lead her but went in circles.

Once she regained her sight, they moved down to the plains. The last three days of the journey they were without food, and when Marie saw smoke ahead, she hid the boys and set out to discover if it was a friendly village. She literally crawled much of the distance to the Walla Wallas' village near present-day Wallula. Men from the village immediately left to back-track her trail and rescue the boys.

A few days later, a group of Astorians came upriver on their way home. They offered to take Marie and the boys back to Saint Louis, but she declined. On hearing her story they estimated that she and the boys spent between 50 and 55 days from the time of Pierre's death until they reached Wallula, more dead than alive.

The men took Marie and the boys upriver to Fort Okanagan, where she married the Canadian Métis Louis Joseph Vernier in 1818, the same year the original Fort

Walla Walla (often referred to as Fort Nez Perce) was built by the British North West Fur Company at Wallula, Washington. She and Vernier had a daughter, Marguerite, sometime between 1819 and 1821.

At some point, Vernier disappears from history, and so far as I know, no records have been found to explain his disappearance. Did he die? Was he killed? Did he tire of the life and return to Canada?

Marie and her family moved back downriver to Fort Walla Walla, where she married again, to John (Jean Baptiste) Toupin, an interpreter and guide. Like her two previous husbands, John was also a metis.

Marie was the factotum, or "woman in charge," of Fort Walla Walla when Marcus and Narcissa Whitman came through in 1836. The Whitmans were missionaries to the Cayuse Indians at that time, and Narcissa Whitman mentioned Marie in her journal, though not by name, as polite, quiet, and unable to speak English. Actually, I think Marie could, and probably did, speak English, though possibly with a French accent.

On 14 April 1838, Marie, her daughter Marguerite Vernier, and Mrs. Pambrun, the wife of the headman at Fort Walla Walla, rode over to the Whitman Mission to visit Narcissa and her little girl, Alice Clarissa. Again, Narcissa mentions in her journal the Indian woman (still nameless) of sweet disposition, who spoke no English. I think Marie didn't want to talk to Narcissa who, by Indian standards, may have spoken in a loud and grating manner.

In 1841, John took a land claim in the Willamette Valley in what became known as French Prairie, outside of Salem, near present-day Champoeg State Park.

On 19 July 1841, Father Francis Norbert Blanchet baptized Marie in the Mission Church of Saint Paul on the Willamette and formally married her and John, adding the prefix, "la," to her tribal name, which then became, in French, Marie La Guivoise.

All Marie's children by Dorion and Vernier, and of course by Toupin, became, in the eyes of the church, legitimized. She named all her children, one by one, for Father Blanchet, and said whether they yet lived or had died. When she got to Paul, she had to stop and think a moment. Was he still alive? He had forsaken her once he was grown—but in those days, at what age was a boy considered a man grown? At age thirteen? At age fifteen? As soon as he reached puberty?

There is little record of Paul; however, he does appear in the William Ashley Company book as "Paul Dorio" [sic] in 1827, and is later reported to have been seen outside Fort Laramie, described by Francis Parkman as, "A shriveled little figure, wrapped from head to foot in a dingy white Canadian capote.... His face was like an old piece of leather, and his mouth spread from ear to ear...." This Paul claimed to be a Dakota (he was Nakota), and the son of Pierre and Marie Dorion. A family member posted online that Paul had gone back east to the Missouri area, married twice, and died in 1889. I took the liberty of making him into a medicine man, though I know of no record indicating that he was.

Once settled in the Willamette Valley, Marie's travels

ceased. She became known as a kind and generous woman who helped any and all of the immigrants who made the long journey and needed help.

Marie died at home on 5 September 1850 and, as a singular honor, was buried inside the parish church, under the steeple, by the parish priest, Father DeLorme.

A special dispensation would have been required for her burial inside the church rather than next to it. Nuns and priests were buried in the church, and I wonder if perhaps Marie was an oblate nun. This status would have allowed her to be buried with the other nuns and priests interred inside the building, but that's a question the answer to which I will probably never know.

The church, a log structure, burned a few years after Marie's burial. Several years after the fire, the old records were found (they were not in the church), and Marie, who had by then been forgotten, was remembered. The exact location of her grave is now unknown, but the church, near present day Champoeg State Park, was rebuilt over the site of the original, and the old graveyard outside the church still exists.

Madame Marie Dorion did not, contrary to an on-going rumor, run a house of ill repute in Pendleton, Oregon—the city wasn't founded until 20 years after her death.

Why was she called Madame Dorion? Because "Madame" is French for our word, "missus."

Appendices

&

Notes

Appendix I
Moons of the Year

Basically, every tribe had names for the moons or months. I decided to use the ones listed online at http://www.inquiry.net/outdoor/native/sign/moons-months.htm This list was compiled by William Tompkins and approved by several tribal members.

January – Snow Moon or Cold Moon

February – Hunger Moon

March – Crow Moon, Awaking Moon, or Warm Moon

April – Grass Moon or Geese Moon

May – Planting Moon or Flower Moon

June – Rose Moon or Buck Moon

July – Heat Moon or Blood Moon

August – Thunder Moon

September – Hunting Moon or Corn Festival Moon

October – Falling Leaf Moon or Traveling Moon

November – Beaver Moon or Mad Moon

December – Long Night Moon

Appendix II
The Hail Mary

Here, first in French and then in English, is the prayer Pierre Dorion said over the baby.

French
Je vous salue, Marie, pleine de grâce.
Le Seigneur est avec vous.
Vous êtes bénie entre toutes les femmes,
et Jésus, le fruit de vos entrailles, est béni.
Sainte Marie, Mère de Dieu,
priez pour nous, pauvres pécheurs,
maintenant et à l'heure de notre mort.
Amen

English
Hail Mary, full of grace,
our Lord is with thee,
blessed art thou among women,
and blessed is the fruit of thy womb, Jesus.
Holy Mary, mother of God,
pray for us sinners,
now, and in the hour of our death.
Amen

Notes by Entry No.

Preface, Fiction Number One

It was common practice for trappers to give their Indian wives names with which they were familiar. French Canadian trappers often chose the names of saints such as Marie for their wives. In all probability, Pierre gave her the name.

No. 3, Corn Festival Moon, 1804

There is no known record of when or where Marie and Pierre were married; most likely it was an Indian wedding, not in a church or with the blessing of the Holy Catholic Church.

No. 4, Corn Festival Moon, 1804

Pierre Dorion, Senior (with his wife Holy Rainbow), is credited with being the first white settler in South Dakota. He built a cabin where the James River flows into the Missouri, near present day Yankton, South Dakota.

No. 7, Flower Moon, 1805

Indian babies were taught from shortly after birth not to cry. A crying baby could alert a nearby enemy to their location, leading to the deaths of many.

No. 8, Flower Moon, 1805

The Carolina parakeet, now extinct, had a large range and was often called a "queet."

No. 10, Strawberry Moon, 1805

"Firewater" is the Indian name for whiskey. The Indians would check the potency by taking a mouthful and spitting it into the fire. If the fire blazed, it was good and deemed "firewater." If the fire did not blaze, it had been watered down and was not good.

No. 24, Cold Moon, 1811

Expedition leaders paid their recruits an advance, up to 50% of the agreed-on salary, so they could buy their supplies before leaving and would pay the remainder at the completion of the journey.

No. 45, 3 June 1811

Sacajawea and her husband left their son, Jean Baptiste, with William Clark to be raised and educated in the ways of the white men in 1809. In 1811, when she and her husband reached Fort Manuel (built by Manuel Lisa), she had another child, a girl, probably in 1812, and died shortly thereafter from the "putrid sickness"—possibly complications in childbirth. A band of Indians attacked the fort, killing many, and Charbonneau was listed among the dead (he was away on a trapping expedition and not killed). Someone brought the baby to Clark, who legally adopted both her and Jean Baptiste according to the records in Saint Louis. The girl lived about a year.

No. 84, 1 October 1811

The Mad River is that part of the Snake River that crashes through and down the mountains below Hoback Junction, Wyoming. Then, it was too rugged for dugout canoes; now, it's a white-water rafting excursion.

Henry's Post, also known as Fort Henry, has been described as two log cabins and a dirt cellar built in 1810–1811 by Andrew Henry and his party. Historians disagree on whether it was two cabins or a bunch of lean-tos and whether it was near present day Saint Anthony, Idaho, or on Conant Creek near Drummond, Idaho. In either case, it was not a fort as was commonly thought of, with a stockade built around it, but a place for trappers to "winter over."

No. 100, 28 October 1811

Today, this sudden narrowing of the Snake River is called the Cauldron Linn, near present-day Burley, Idaho. The river narrowed quickly, and before the men could react, four canoes shot over the waterfall and fell 25 feet, to the churning waters and whirlpool below.

No. 111, 10 November 1811

We now know the soil on that plain is very thin and the rocks very porous. Rain goes right through them until the water reaches an impermeable layer and then works its way to the edge of the gorge where it falls, starting a distance below the canyon top.

No. 113, 12 November 1811

These dogs were working dogs, used for labor and protein. They were not pets. Dog was a primary source of meat, and white men, including the men of Lewis and Clark's expedition, often preferred it to the rich and oily salmon on a day-to-day diet, especially the salmon that had traveled far up the Columbia and Snake Rivers and was pretty well beat by the time it was caught.

No. 128, 28 November 1811

The Great Falls of the Columbia were known to the local people as the Celilo Falls, near The Dalles, Oregon. The falls are now covered by Celilo Lake, which was created by The Dalles Dam.

No. 142, 16 December 1811

They had just tried to hike what today is known as Hell's Canyon.

No. 147, 23 December 1811

This is the day they departed present-day Farewell

Bend, Oregon State Park.

No. 151, 31 December 1811

The baby is never identified by anyone on the trip either by gender or name. Historians have decided and agreed it was a boy.

No. 155, 7 January 1812

No one knows where the baby is buried. My best guess is near the top of McKay Creek Canyon, not too far from present-day Emigrant Springs State Park, Oregon.

No. 193, 28 August 1813

Scrofula is a swelling of the glands, a form of tuberculosis. And a painful way to die.

No 198, Cold Moon, 1814

There is discussion on the term "Dog-Rib." There is no known tribe or clan of the Snake Indians, and it is possible Marie did not hear it correctly or it was a pejorative used by the man who told her.

PARTIAL BIBLIOGRAPHY

Partial Bibliography

Dillon, Richard [2003], *Meriwether Lewis, A Biography*, Great West Books, Lafayette, California

Dorion, Leonard, "Pierre Dorion II" online at: http://users.usinternet.com/dfnels/dorion.htm

Eddins, O. Ned, "Overland Astorians Across the Rocky Mountains To The Oregon Country," http://www.thefurtrapper.com/wilson_hunt.htm

Eddins, O. Ned, "The Astorians and the Pacific Fur Company," online at: http://www.thefurtrapper.com/

Eddins, Orland Ned [2009], *The Winds of Change*, Peczuh Printing Company, Price, Utah

Faircloth, Michael, Sr., editor [2010], *Madame Marie Dorion – Idaho's First Heroine*, Snake River Outpost No. 1811 and the Canyon County Historical Society, Boise, Idaho

Frazier Farmstead Museum, Courtesy of, "Pierre Dorion II," genealogy online at: http://tinyurl.com/jwuufw6

Hunt, Wilson Price, English Translation of his *Nouvelles Annales de Voyages* from Hunt's journal http://user.xmission.com/~drudy/mtman/html/

Irving, Washington [2007], *Astoria,* The Echo Library, Teddington, Middlesex

Jewett, Wayne [2000], "Marie Dorion and The Astoria Expedition" by *Wild West Magazine*; printed online June 12, 2006, historynet.com/marie-dorion-and-the-astoria-expedition.htm

Lavender, David [1964], *The Fist in the Wilderness*, University of Nebraska Press, Lincoln and London

"Marie Aioe Dorion," published online without attribution at: http://en.wikipedia.org/wiki/Marie_Aioe_Dorion

"Marie Dorion (1786 – 1850)" taken from *Young and Brave: Girls Changing History*, published online by National Women's History Museum at: http://tinyurl.com/n3lwby9

"Marie Dorion," Oregon State Historical Marker, published without attribution online at: web.oregon.com/history/hm/marie_Dorion.cfm

"Marie Dorion," published online by Women of the Fur Trade without attribution at: womenofthefurtrade.com/Marie_Dorion.html

"Marie Dorion Dam Removal," information collected by Kristin Keith, published online by Wild Fish Habitat Initiative at: http://tinyurl.com/kd5zv3a

Mountain Men and Life in the Rocky Mountain West, Malachite's Big Hole. "Marie Dorion," published online, without attribution at: http://www.mman.us/Dorionswife.htm

National Park Service, "Arikara," Jefferson National Expansion Memorial, online at:

http://www.nps.gov/jeff/historyculture/

Peck, David J., D.O. [2002], Or Perish in the Attempt, Wilderness Medicine in the Lewis & Clark Expedition, Farcountry Press, Helena, MT

Peltier, Jerome ed. by Edward J. Kowrach [1980], *Madame Dorion*, Ye Galleon Press, Fairfield, Washington

Ruby, Robert H., and John A. Brown [1972], *The Cayuse Indians, Imperial Tribesmen of Old Oregon*, University of Oklahoma Press, Norman OK

Schoenbert, Wilfred P., S. J. [1987], *A History of the Catholic Church in the Pacific Northwest 1743–1983*, Pastoral Press, Washington, D.C.

Stuart, Robert ed. by Philip Aston Rollins [1935], The Discovery of the Oregon Trail — Robert Stuart's Narratives of His Overland Trip Eastward from Astoria in 1812–1813, University of Nebraska Press, Lincoln and London.

Utley, Robert M. [1997], A Life Wild and Perilous: Mountain Men and the Paths to the Pacific, Henry Holt and Company, New York

Whitman, Narcissa [2004], *My Journal*, Ye Galleon Press, Fairfield, Washington.

About the Artist:

Leah Marie Dorion

Leah Marie Dorion is a direct descendant of Jean Baptist Dorion! She is an Indigenous (Metis) interdisciplinary artist raised in Prince Albert, Saskatchewan, Canada. She is a self-taught visual artist and credits her creative family for inspiring her to take up painting and the traditional Metis arts. Leah is also a teacher, published author, and storyteller. Her art pays homage to women, earth based spirituality, and the Indigenous knowledge.

Visit **www.leahdorion.ca** for more information about her artistic practice.

The cover art on this book, "Michif Women Packers" was created and dedicated to Madame Marie Dorion in 2011 by Leah Marie Dorion.

About The Author:

Lenora Rain-Lee Good

Born and raised in Portland, Oregon, Lenora Rain-Lee Good has lived most of her life in the Great Pacific Northwest. She had some marvelous teachers who gave her a love of history, especially the history of her native state, Oregon.

She served as a WAC in the Deep South and Germany where she was stationed at Karlsruhe—the only WAC in town. Following her retirement from The Boeing Company in Seattle, she moved to warmer Florida for one year and 51 weeks. Her house was located close enough to a waterway that she could hear the 'gators roaring in season. Armadillos roamed through her yard at night, snakes came up on her patio, and she experienced, first-hand, a Category 5 hurricane.

Lenora moved again, this time to *truly* sunny *and dry* Kennewick, Washington, where she is happily at home with her cat, Tashiko Akuma Pestini, and faithful muse. When she's not writing, she's quilting, or reading. She has recently moved into a condo, which informed her the name of her new home is The House of Frog and Dragon. She admits she spends way too much time visiting online, by phone, or in person with her many friends—and simultaneously doing research for her next writing project.

Lenora has sold three young adult novels, *My*

Adventures as Brother Rat, a novel of Ancient China; *Jiang Li: Warrior Woman of Yueh*, another novel of Ancient China; and *Yadh, the Ugly*, a fantasy. She also writes radio plays, short stories, and poems. She loves to travel, photographing the landscapes she visits.

In fact, Lenora traveled the overland route from the present-day Mobridge, South Dakota (near the three Arikara villages) to Astoria, Oregon, keeping as close as possible to the route Marie travelled. Interestingly, the present I-84 follows Marie's route across Idaho and Oregon. Photographs from this trip have been compiled into a slide show or trailer, which can be viewed at either of the following websites:

https://youtu.be/FaAUyAqjnFM

https://youtu.be/P9oLW8VkYLA

Lenora loves to hear from her readers! Her phone line is nearly always busy, but she can be reached quite easily via email at lenora.good@icloud.com.

You can find out more on her website and through her blog at **lenorarainleegood.com**.

Acknowledgments

There are so many people I need to thank, and I fear I shall inadvertently leave someone out, but to all of you, I offer my heartfelt gratitude, special thanks, and profound apologies. In particular, gratitude goes to:

My Sister of Choice, Marjorie Rommel, who is one of my most devout fans, prods me when I despair, and will not let me be lazy or sloppy in my writing. I hereby acknowledge you, Sis. Without you, I would never have made it.

My new friend, O. Ned Eddins, a modern-day mountain man, who also writes and runs the web site http://www.thefurtrapper.com/fur_trappers.htm and gave generously of his time and expertise, answering all my questions (and there were many), and offering much encouragement. I hope, someday, we can meet face to face. In the meantime, I give him my heartiest of thanks.

Judith Whitehead, who made the road trip with me, driving Marie's path as closely as possible, and kept me entertained by reading, aloud, interesting information from the Roadside Geology books she brought. A marvelous travel companion! A big thanks for the fun, the laughs, and for not letting me nap while driving.

My readers, who read, gave helpful comments, and have repeatedly saved me from falling flat on my face: Judy Arndt, Tara Swanson, Richard Badalamente, Ann Roseberry, Judith Whitehead, Marcus Spaur.

The various historians who responded to my queries about place names both then and now—especially Loren Yellow Bird, who solved a great mystery for me.

A most special thank you to Seth Dalby, Director, Archives & Records Management, Catholic Archdiocese of Seattle, who answered many questions about this book and another, and put me onto one of the best resource books ever!

And a huge debt of gratitude goes to Jane Kirkpatrick, who not only read an earlier version but also gave valuable insight and comments, as well as her endorsement!

Last, but definitely not least, is my publisher, Dixiane Hallaj, of S & H Publishing, who had the faith and the courage to publish this second version of *Madame Dorion: Her Journey to the Oregon Country.*